THE SECRET OF
CLIFF CASTLE

Enid Blyton ®

THE SECRET OF
CLIFF CASTLE

Bounty
Books

First published 1947, 1943 and 1963 as *The Secret of Cliff Castle*,
Smuggler Ben and *The Boy Who Wanted a Dog*

Published in 2014 by Bounty Books,
a division of Octopus Publishing Group Ltd,
Endeavour House,
189 Shaftesbury Avenue,
London WC2H 8JY
www.octopusbooks.co.uk

An Hachette UK Company
www.hachette.co.uk
Enid Blyton ® Text copyright © 1947, 1943, 1963, 2014 Hodder &
Stoughton Ltd.
Illustrations copyright © 2014 Octopus Publishing Group Ltd.
Layout copyright © 2014 Octopus Publishing Group Ltd.

Illustrated by Maggie Downer.
Cover illustration by Laurence Whiteley.

ISBN: 978-0-75372-703-4

A CIP catalogue record for this book is available from the
British Library.

Printed and bound in Spain

CONTENTS

THE SECRET OF
CLIFF CASTLE

1

Off for a Holiday

Peter and Pam leaned out of the railway carriage together and waved goodbye to their mother as their train slowly left the long platform.

"Goodbye, Mum! Goodbye!"

"Be good!" called Mother. "Goodbye! Have a lovely holiday! Give my love to Auntie Hetty."

"I hope Brock will be at the station to meet us," said Peter. "Good old Brock. It will be lovely to see his smiling face again."

Brock was their cousin. They were going to stay with him for part of the summer holidays, down in the country village of Rockhurst. Usually they went to the sea, but this summer their mother thought it would be nice for them to be in the country. Then Auntie Hetty had phoned to invite them for three weeks, and the children had been thrilled.

"We can go to the farm and see all the new animals there," said Pam. "And we can go exploring in the woods and find exciting things there. I hope there are some woods near."

"There are always woods in the country," said Peter. "Anyway, Brock will know all the places to go to. It's fun going to a place we've never been to before!"

The train sped on. It soon left London behind, and green fields took the place of houses and streets. The train was an express, and stopped at very few stations. The children had sandwiches with them, and when Pam's wristwatch showed half past twelve, Peter undid the parcel their mother had handed them, and took out the packets of food.

"I always feel so hungry in a train, somehow," said Pam. "Oooh – ham sandwiches. How lovely! What's in that other packet, Peter?"

"Biscuits, and two pieces of cake," said Peter looking to see. "Oh, and two bars of chocolate as well. What a nice lunch. Mum's put in some lemonade, too – it's in that bag, Pam. Get it down."

Pam reached down the leather bag in which Mother had squeezed a bottle of lemonade and two cardboard cups. Soon the two children were eating a lovely lunch, watching the scenery as it flew by the carriage window.

"We shall arrive at Rockhurst at half past three," said Peter. "But we've got to change at Deane. We must look out for that."

It was quite easy to change at Deane. They heard the announcement, "Change here for Rockhurst! Change here for Rockhurst," and out the children hopped with their suitcases. The little train for Rockhurst stood on the other side of the platform, and they simply got out of one train and into the other! It was fun.

"Won't be long now," said Peter. "You know, Pam, I feel awfully excited. I feel as if we're going to have adventures!"

"I feel that too," said Pam. "But I usually do feel like that when I'm setting out on a holiday."

"So do I," said Peter. "But this time I feel we really are. Proper adventures, I mean. Sort of dangerous, you know!"

"Do you really?" said Pam, feeling all excited too. "Oooh, I hope we do have some; I'd like some. School was so dull last term that I could do with something exciting in the hols!"

"Goodness! Isn't it slow, after the express!" said Pam. "We could almost lean out of the window and pick flowers off the bank!"

Peter laughed. "Well, in another twenty minutes we shall be there," he said. "And then we'll see old Brock."

The time went by, and at exactly half past three the little train drew in at a small country platform, where red geraniums flared in beds at the back. It was Rockhurst.

Peter jumped out and helped Pam down. She looked eagerly up and down the platform, while Peter dragged out the two suitcases and the big leather bag. Pam gave a shriek.

"Oh! There's Brock! Brock! Brock! Here we are! Hello!"

Brock came rushing up. He was a tall boy with a strong body and a brown, smiling face. His eyes shone very blue in the sunshine as he greeted his cousins. He was twelve, the same age as Peter, but stronger and taller. Pam was ten, smaller than either of the boys.

Brock clapped his cousins on the back, and grinned at them. "Hello! Glad to see you both! Welcome to Rockhurst!"

"Hello!" said Peter, smiling. "It's good to see you, Brock. Gosh, you've grown awfully tall since we saw you last year. You make me look quite small."

"Come on," said Brock, taking one of the suitcases. "Mother's outside with the car."

They gave up their tickets and went out of the station, chattering hard. Pam called out to her aunt, in delight, "Hello, Aunt Hetty! Here we are! It is nice of you to come and meet us."

"Hello, my dears," said their aunt. "Glad to see you. Climb in. Brock, put the cases in the boot."

Soon the four of them were driving along the country lanes. The sun shone down, and everything looked bright and holiday-like. The children felt very happy.

They soon arrived at Brock's home. It was a comfortable-looking house, rather rambling, set in a nice big garden. The children liked the look of it very much.

"It's a friendly sort of house, isn't it?" said Pam. "Oh, Aunt Hetty, isn't the beginning of a holiday exciting?"

"Very exciting!" said their aunt. "Quite the most exciting part of a holiday, I always think."

"But it isn't going to be the most exciting part of this holiday!" said Peter, as the car came to a standstill in front of the house. "I've got a funny feeling about this holiday. It's going to be exciting all the way through!"

"What do you mean?" asked Brock in surprise.

"I don't exactly know," said Peter, jumping out, and helping his aunt. "But I've got a feeling! You just wait and see!"

"Well, I hope your feeling is right!" said Brock, and they all went into the house.

2

A Little Exploring

Tea was ready when they got indoors. The children washed their hands and brushed their hair. Peter was sharing Brock's little room, and Pam had a tiny room to herself up in the attic. She loved it because it had peculiar slanting ceilings, and funny uneven boards in the floor. She looked out of the window as she brushed her hair, humming a little tune to herself because she was so happy.

The countryside lay smiling in the afternoon sunshine. Cottages clustered together here and there, and cattle grazed in the fields. In the distance, a curious, steep hill caught her eye. It rose up very suddenly, and at the top was a strange building. It looked like a small square castle, for it had towers at each end.

"I wonder if anyone lives there," thought Pam. "It looks sort of deserted, somehow. I'll ask Brock about it."

Downstairs, round the tea table, Brock and his cousins chattered nineteen to the dozen about everything, telling each other all their news. Aunt

Hetty smiled as she listened, and handed round her plates of home-made scones with jam, and new ginger buns, and currant pastries.

"Anyone would think you hadn't had anything to eat since breakfast-time," she said, as one after another the plates were emptied.

"Well, we did have a good lunch on the train," said Peter, "but it seems ages ago now. I do like these buns, Aunt Hetty. They're the nicest I've ever tasted."

"Shall we go out and explore round a bit, after tea?" said Pam. "I'm longing to. I saw the farm not far off, Brock – and what is that strange sort of castle on the top of that very steep hill towards the west?"

"Oh, that's Cliff Castle," said Brock. "It's called that because it's built on that steep hill, which falls away behind the castle in a kind of cliff."

"Does anyone live there?" asked Peter.

"Not now," said Brock. "Mum, who lived there, years ago?"

"Oh, I don't really know," said his mother. "It belonged to a strange old man who wanted to live quite alone. So he built himself that castle and lived there with two old servants as strange as himself. He spent a fortune on the castle. When he died, he left a will which said the castle was to be left

16

exactly as it was, cared for by the two old servants till they died. Then it was to go to some great-nephew, who has never bothered to live there – or even to go and visit the castle, as far as I know."

"Is it really a castle?" said Pam.

"No, not really," said Aunt Hetty. "But it's built to appear like one, as you see – and I believe the walls are almost as thick as a real old castle's would be. People do say that there are secret passages in it, but I don't believe that. What would a lonely old man want with secret passages! That's just make believe."

The children stared out of the window at the lonely castle on the top of the steep hill. It suddenly seemed very mysterious and exciting to them. It stood there with the sinking sun behind it, and looked rather black and forbidding.

"Is it quite empty then, Aunt Hetty?" asked Pam.

"Quite," said her aunt. "It must be a dreadful mess by now, too, I should think, for nobody has dusted it for years, or lit a fire there to warm the place. The furniture must be mouldy and rotten. Not a nice place to visit at all!"

Peter and Pam looked at one another. It seemed to them that their aunt was quite wrong. It would be a wonderfully exciting place to visit! If only they could!

After tea, they spoke to Brock about it. "Brock! Will you take us to see Cliff Castle one day soon? Tomorrow, perhaps. It does sound so exciting and it looks so strange and lonely. We'd simply love to explore round about it."

"We'll go tomorrow!" said Brock. "But come and see our garden now, and the farm. We've plenty of time."

So the three of them went over to the big garden and admired the vegetables, the outdoor tomatoes, the peaches on the wall, and everything. They saw Brock's exciting playhouse in the garden, too, set all by itself out of sight of the house.

"Dad had this built for me to take my friends to, when we wanted to play by ourselves," said Brock. "You know, Mum doesn't like a lot of noise, and boys can't help being rowdy, can they? So I just take my friends to my playhouse when we want a good old game – and we don't disturb Mum a bit! We can play out here on rainy days, too. It will be fun."

Peter and Pam liked Brock's playhouse. It was a small, sturdy, little wooden house with a red door, and windows each side. Inside there was one big room, and round it were spread all Brock's possessions – a small radio, a big Meccano set, boxes and boxes of railway lines, engines, trucks, signals, and other things belonging to a railway – and on a bookshelf were scores of exciting-looking books.

"You are lucky, Brock!" said Peter, looking round. "This is a lovely place."

"Yes – we'll come here and talk when we want to be all by ourselves," said Brock. "Nobody can see us or hear us. It's our own private place."

They went to see the farm, too, and then the sun sank so low that it was time to go back home to supper. The strange castle on the hill showed up clearly as they went down the farm lane back to their house.

"Brock, do take us to Cliff Castle tomorrow," said Peter. "It would be marvellous fun to explore it. Haven't you ever been there yourself?"

"I haven't been very near it," said Brock. "I somehow never liked the look of it very much, you know. I think it's got rather an evil look!"

"It has, rather," said Peter. "Anyway, do let's go tomorrow!"

"All right," said Brock. "I shan't mind going with you – though I've never wanted to go alone!"

It was fun going to bed that night in a strange bedroom. The two boys talked till late, and Brock's mother had to go in twice to stop them.

Pam could hear their voices as she lay in bed,

and she wished she was with the two boys so that she might hear what they said.

She fell asleep, and did not wake until the house was all in a bustle with its early morning cleaning. She heard the two boys talking below in loud voices and she jumped out of bed at once.

"It's holiday-time – and we're at Brock's – and we're going exploring today!" she hummed to herself, as she dressed quickly. She ran downstairs to breakfast feeling very hungry.

"What are you going to do today?" asked Aunt Hetty, pouring out the tea.

"We're going over to Cliff Castle," said Brock. "Can we take sandwiches, Mum, and have a picnic?"

"All right," said his mother. "You must all make your beds, and tidy your rooms, please, before you go. I'll get you some lunch ready while you do that."

It wasn't long after breakfast before the three children were ready to set out. Brock's mother had been very generous with the picnic lunch. She had cut them meat sandwiches, tomato sandwiches, and egg sandwiches, and had put some buttered scones, some ginger buns, and some boiled sweets into the packets, too.

"There's a tiny shop not far from Cliff Castle

where you can buy yourselves something to drink," she said. "Here is some money for that. Now – off you go!"

They set off happily. Brock knew the way, though it was rather a roundabout one, down narrow little lanes, through a small wood, and then across some fields. It was eleven o'clock by the time they got to the little shop where they wanted to buy drinks.

"I'm so thirsty already that I could drink about twelve bottles of lemonade straight off!" said Peter.

"Well, don't let's drink all of it straightaway," said Brock. "The woman here has a well. Look, there it is, with the bucket beside it. Let's ask her if we can have a drink of cold water – then we can save up the lemonade!"

The woman said that of course they could use her well water. "Have a whole bucketful, if you like!" she said. But they couldn't quite manage that. They sent down the bucket, and it came up filled with silvery water.

"It's absolutely ice-cold!" said Pam, gasping a little at the coldness. "But it's simply lovely."

"Where are you off to?" asked the woman, handing them three small bottles of lemonade.

"To explore round about Cliff Castle," said Peter.

"Oh, I wouldn't do that," said the woman.

"Really, I wouldn't. It's a strange place. And people do say that funny lights have been seen there lately. Well, that's very strange, isn't it, in a place that's been empty for years?"

"Most peculiar," said Brock, staring at the woman and feeling rather excited. "What sort of lights?"

"I don't know," said the woman. "I only know I wouldn't go near that place in the dark, or in the daytime either! There's always been something odd about it – and there is still!"

The children said goodbye and went out of the tiny dark shop. They stared up at the nearby hill, on the top of which stood Cliff Castle. It looked much bigger now that they were near it. It had funny little slit-like windows, just like very old castles had. It certainly was a peculiar place for anyone to build in days when castles were no longer of any use!

"Well, come on," said Brock, at last. "Don't let's be put off by silly village stories. Mum says stories always get made up about any deserted place."

"They certainly make it more exciting," said Peter, hitching his rucksack full of lunch over his shoulder. "Well – up the hill we go!"

And up the hill they went. There was no proper road up the steep hill, only a small, narrow path

that wound between jutting-out rocks, for it was a very rocky part of the countryside. Stunted bushes grew on the hillside, mostly of gorse. It was exposed to the east winds, and nothing very much grew there.

"Well – here we are!" said Brock, at last. "Cliff Castle! I wonder what we shall find there."

3

Cliff Castle

Now that the children were right up to the castle, it looked enormous! It rose up in front of them, square and sturdy, a tower at each end. Its small, slit-like windows had no glass in. The great front door was studded with big nails that had gone rusty. There was a large knocker, which the children longed to use – but which, of course, they dared not touch!

"Let's go all the way round the castle and see what we can see," said Pam.

So they went down the great flight of steps again, and began to make their way round the towering walls of the strange castle. It was difficult, because creepers, bushes and weeds grew high up the walls. Tall nettles stood in great patches, and the children had to make their way round them after Pam was badly stung on her bare legs.

"We'll find some dock leaves to help the stings," said Peter, and he found a patch of dark green dock leaves. He picked some and Pam pressed the cool leaves against her burning skin.

"That's better," she said. "Gracious, I shan't go near nettles again today!"

They went on their way round the great grey walls. The slit-like windows were placed at regular intervals. The children gazed up at them.

"You know, in the olden days, they had those funny narrow windows so that archers could shoot their arrows out without being hit themselves," said Brock rather learnedly. "I can't imagine why the old man should have built windows like that for himself, long after the time of bows and arrows had gone! It must make the rooms inside very dark."

"I wish we could see them, don't you?" said Pam excitedly. "Just imagine how strange they would look after all these years when nobody has been here – cobwebs all over the place – dust everywhere. Oooh – it would be very odd."

They could not go all round the castle, because, when they came to the side that faced due west, the hill fell away so steeply that it was impossible to go any further. The walls of the castle were built almost sheer with the hillside, and there was a very big drop down to the bottom of the hills below.

"Let's have our lunch now," said Peter, all at once feeling terribly hungry. "It's almost time. We can find a nice place out of the hot sun and sit down, can't we?"

"Rather!" said Brock, feeling hungry too. "Look – what about that shady bit over there, facing the castle? We can look at the castle while we're eating."

They sat down in the shady spot and undid all they had to eat. It had seemed a lot when Brock's mother had packed it up – but it didn't seem nearly so much when three hungry children began to eat it. They unscrewed the tops of the lemonade bottles and drank eagerly. Except that the lemonade was a little warm, it was delicious.

Pam finished her lunch first, because she did not want as much as the boys, and gave some of hers to them to finish up. She lay back against a tree and looked up at the silent grey castle.

She looked at the narrow windows and began to count them. When she came to the second row, she spoke out loud: "Look, Peter; look, Brock – there's a window in the second row up that is bigger than the others. I wonder why."

The boys looked up. Peter screwed up his eyes to see why the window should be bigger.

"I don't think it's meant to be bigger," he said, at last. "I think the weather has sort of eaten it away. It looks to me as if the bottom part of it has crumbled away. Perhaps a pipe comes out just there, and has leaked down the window and made the stone and brickwork rotten."

"Do you see the tree that grows up to that window?" said Brock, in sudden excitement. "I believe we could climb it and look in at that window! I wonder what we should see if we did!"

Peter and Pam stared at him, and then at the tree that grew up to the window. What fun it would be if they really could climb it and have a peep inside the castle!

"Well, let's see if we can peep inside any of the lower windows first," said Peter. "I don't think Aunt Hetty would be very pleased with us if we climbed trees in these clothes. We really want old clothes for that."

"Oh, bother our clothes!" said Brock, his brown face shining with excitement. "I vote we climb up! But we'll have a peep in at one of the lower windows first. Peter, you come and give me a leg up."

It wasn't long before Peter was bending down, heaving Brock up to the narrow windowsill to see inside the slit-like window. Brock peered through, but could see nothing at all.

"It's so dark inside," he said. "It wouldn't be so bad if the sun wasn't so brilliant today – but my eyes just simply can't see a thing inside the darkness of the castle."

"Well, we'll climb the tree then!" cried Pam, running to it. She loved climbing trees as much as the boys did.

"Wait a bit, Pam," cried Brock. "Peter and I will go up first and give you a hand. You're only a girl, you know."

It always made Pam cross to be told she was only a girl. "I'm as strong as you are, anyway!" she cried, and looked about for an easy way to climb.

But Brock was up the tree before either of the others. He was a country boy, used to climbing, and he saw at once the best way to go up. He was soon lost to sight among the greenery.

His voice came down to them: "Go up the way I did. It's not difficult."

Peter followed him, and then Pam. Pam had to have a hand from Peter every now and again, and she was glad of it. They were soon all of them up on a high branch beside Brock. He grinned at them.

"Good climbing!" he said. "Now, look – see this branch? It reaches right to that window. It's pretty strong, and I think it will bear us all. But we'd better go one at a time, in case it doesn't."

"You go first, then," said Peter.

Brock edged his way along the branch, working carefully with his arms and legs. The bough bent beneath his weight and swung down below the windowsill. Brock came back.

"No good," he said. "We'll try the next branch. That looks a good deal stronger – and although it grows right above the window at its tip, our weight will bend it down till it rests almost on the windowsill, I should think."

They all climbed a little higher. Then Brock worked his way along the next branch. As he said, his weight bent it gradually down, and by the time he was at the end of it, its tip rested on the sill itself. Part of it even went right through the window-opening into the castle.

"Good!" said Brock. He put one leg across the stone windowsill, and peered into the slit. He could see nothing but darkness. But certainly the weather had worn away the stone around that window, for the opening was almost big enough to take Brock's body!

"I believe I could get right inside!" he called to the others. He stood upright on the sill and tried to work his way in. It was a very tight fit, for Brock was not thin! He had to squeeze himself in till he almost burst.

He found that the wall was very thick — about a metre thick, before he had got right through the window. Then he jumped down to the floor inside and called out through the slit. "Come on! It's not very difficult! We'll be able to explore the castle from top to bottom, if you can get through!"

4

Inside the Castle

Pam felt a little nervous about going right into the castle, but she couldn't hold back if the boys thought it was all right. So she followed Peter when he squeezed himself through the slit in the stone walls, and held his hand tightly when he gave it to her to jump down into the darkness.

Two slit-like windows lit the room they were in. It seemed as dark as night to the children when they first looked round but their eyes soon grew accustomed to it, and they began to see quite well. Shafts of bright sunlight lit up the room in two places – the rest seemed rather dark.

They stared round, and then Pam cried out in disappointment: "Oh – the room is empty! It's just like a prison cell! There's absolutely nothing here!"

She was right. There was nothing to see at all, except for bare walls, bare floor, and bare ceiling. At the far side was a closed door, big and strong. It had an iron handle. Brock went over to it.

"Well, we may be unlucky in this room, finding nothing to see," he said, "but maybe there will be plenty to see somewhere else! Let's open this door and explore!"

He pulled at the door by the great iron handle. It opened! Outside was a dark passage. Brock felt in his pockets, remembering that he had a torch somewhere. He found it and switched it on.

The passage led from a narrow stone stairway, and seemed to wind round a corner. "Come on," said Brock. "This way! We'll open a few doors and see what there is to be seen."

He opened a door nearby. But again there was nothing to be seen but bareness. He shut the door, and the noise echoed through the stone castle in a very strange way. It sounded as though dozens of doors were being shut, one after another. Pam shivered.

"Oooh!" she said. "It's not nice to make a noise in this place. Even a little sound echoes round like thunder."

No room just there had anything in it at all. It was most disappointing. Brock then led the way to the stone staircase. It wound downwards in the heart of the castle, and as it came towards the bottom, grew a little wider.

It ended in a vast room with an enormous fireplace at one end. "This must be the kitchen," said Pam in surprise. "And I suppose those stairs we came down were the back stairs. There must be a bigger flight somewhere else. I did think they were very narrow stairs for such a huge place."

The kitchen was furnished. There was a big wooden table, and round it were set stout wooden chairs. Pots and pans hung round the stove. There was an iron pot hanging over what had once been a fire. Brock peered into it. There was an evil-smelling dark liquid in it.

"Something made by witches!" he said, in a deep, mournful voice that made Pam jump. Brock laughed. "It's all right," he said. "It's only soup or something, gone bad after all these years!"

The kitchen was dark and dirty, and there was not much to be seen there. The children went out of it and came into a great hall from which four doors led off. Brock opened one.

And then, indeed, there was something to be seen! The big room beyond the door was furnished most magnificently! Great couches, carved chairs, cabinets, tables – all these stood about the room just as they had been left! But how mournful they looked, for they were adorned with spiders' webs, and when the children walked into the room, clouds of fine grey dust flew up from their feet.

Sunlight came in long golden shafts through four of the slit-like windows, and divided the room into quarters. It made the whole room even stranger than it might have been, for the brilliance of the sunlight lay in sharp contrast to the blackness of the shadows in the far corners.

"Oooh! What an enormous spider!" said Pam, with a shudder, as a great long-legged spider ran out from under a table. The boys didn't mind spiders. They didn't even mind walking into the cobwebs that hung here and there from the enormous chandeliers that had once lit the room. But Pam couldn't bear the strange, light touch of the webs on her hair, and longed to get out into the sunshine again.

"Isn't it odd, to have left everything just like this?" said Brock wonderingly. "Look at those curtains. They must once have been simply gorgeous but now they are all faded and dusty."

He touched one and it fell to pieces in his hand. It was almost as if someone had breathed on it and made it melt!

"The brocade on the furniture is all rotten, too," said Pam, as she felt it. It shredded away under her fingers. "Everything is moth-eaten. What a horrid, sad place this feels. I don't like it. Let's get away."

"No – we'll explore first," said Peter. "Don't be a spoilsport, Pam. Come with us. You'll be quite all right."

Pam didn't want to be a spoilsport, so she followed the boys rather unwillingly as they went out of the room and into the next.

The same things were found there – furniture and curtains, rotten and decayed. A musty smell hung over everything. It was most unpleasant. Pam began to feel sick.

"I hate this smell," she said, " and I hate walking into these nasty webs. I can't seem to see them and it's horrid to get them all round my head."

"Let's go upstairs again," said Brock. "And this time we'll go up by the main stairway – look, that great flight of steps over there – not by the little narrow back staircase we came down."

They mounted the enormous stone steps, and came to some big rooms furnished as bedrooms. Up they went again and came to more rooms. Leading out of one of them was a tiny staircase all on its own. It wound up into one of the stone towers that stood at the end of the castle.

"Let's go up this staircase!" cried Peter. "We shall get a marvellous view over the countryside!"

So up they went and came to the open door of a strange, square little room that seemed to be cut right out of the heart of the tower. A tiny slit on each side let in the light. A stone bench ran round the walls, but otherwise there was nothing in the room.

"What a wonderful view!" cried Pam, peering out of one of the slits. She saw the whole of the countryside to the east lying smiling in the hot August sun. It looked marvellous.

"I can see our house!" cried Brock. "Over there, beyond the farm. Oh, how tiny it looks! And how small the cows and horses look, too. Like animals on a toy farm."

So they did. It was fun to peer out and see everything from so high up. But soon the children grew tired of it and thought they would go downstairs again.

So down they went, and then paused on the first floor where they had first squeezed in through the window. But somehow they couldn't find the room they had climbed inside! It was strange. They opened door after door, but no, there wasn't a tree outside a window.

"I've lost my bearings," said Peter, at last. "I've no idea where that room was. Well, if we don't want to stay here all night we've got to get out somehow! I vote we go right downstairs into the hall, then make our way to the kitchen, and up that back stairway again. We know the room was somewhere near the top of that."

So down they went into the hall, into the kitchen, and then towards the back stairway.

But just near the stairway was a small door, very low, set in the wall. The children stared at it. They hadn't noticed it before.

"Perhaps we could open this and get out by it," said Peter. "It would save us all that big climb down the tree. I tried the front door to see if we could get out by that, but it was much too heavy. The bolts had all rusted into the door, and I couldn't even turn the handle. Let's try this funny little door."

"It's so low we'll have to bend down to get out of it!" said Brock, with a laugh. They went to the little door and looked at it. It was latched on the inside, but not bolted or locked, though the key stood in the door. Peter lifted the latch.

After a push, the door opened a little way, and then stuck fast. The two boys together pushed hard. It opened just a little further, and sunshine came through.

Peter put his head round the edge. "There's a great patch of nettles and a gorse bush preventing it from opening," he said. "Got a knife, Brock? I believe if I hacked away at this gorse bush a bit I could make the door open enough to let us out!"

Brock passed him a fierce-looking knife. Peter hacked at the bush, and cut off the pieces that were stopping the door from opening. "Cut away the nettles, too," begged Pam. "My legs still sting from that other patch we went into."

Peter did his best. Then he and Brock were able to push the door open just enough to let them squeeze through one by one. They were all rather glad to be standing out in the bright sunshine again, after the dim, musty darkness of the silent castle.

"I say – if we just push this door to, and leave it like that, not locked or bolted, we shall be able to get in whenever we want to!" said Peter. "We might find it rather fun to come and play smugglers or something here. We could pile weeds against the door so that nobody else would notice it."

"Good idea!" said Brock. So they shut the door gently, then forced the gorse bush back against it, and pulled pieces from a nearby hedge to throw against the door to hide it.

Pam got stung again by the nettles, and almost cried with the pain. Peter had to hunt for dock leaves again!

"Cheer up!" he said. "What do a few nettle-stings matter? We've had quite an adventure this afternoon! We'll come back here again soon and have a great time."

Pam wasn't sure she wanted to. But she didn't say so! The boys talked eagerly about the afternoon's excitement on the way home – and by the time they reached the house, Pam had begun to think that nettle-stings or no nettle-stings, it had all been simply marvellous!

5

In the Middle of the Night

The next day Aunt Hetty took Pam and Peter and their cousin Brock to the sea, which was about three miles away. This was such fun that the three children forgot all about Cliff Castle for a day or two. And then something happened that reminded them of it.

It was something that happened in the middle of the night. Pam woke up and felt very thirsty. She remembered that Aunt Hetty had left a jug of water and a tumbler on the chest-of-drawers and she got up to get it.

She stood at the window, drinking the water. It was a moonlit night, but the moon kept going behind clouds. It showed up Cliff Castle very clearly, when it shone down. But when it went behind the clouds the castle was just a black mass on the hill.

Then Pam saw something flickering quickly somewhere at the top of the castle. It caught her eye for a second and then disappeared. What could it be?

She stood watching the castle, forgetting to drink the cool water. Then the flicker came again, this time further down the castle. Then it disappeared once more. It came for the third and last time at the bottom.

Pam felt excited. She remembered what the woman at the little shop had said about strange lights being seen in the castle. Now here they were again — and they were real, because Pam had seen them!

"I really must wake the boys and tell them!" she thought. "I know it isn't a dream now but in the morning I might think it was, and not tell them. But it isn't a dream, I've seen the lights!"

She crept down the stairs and into the open door of the boys' room. They were both sleeping peacefully. Pam shook Peter and he woke with a jump.

"What is it?" he said loudly, sitting up in bed, surprised to see that it was night.

"Sh!" said Pam. "It's me, Peter. Listen — I got up to get a drink of water and I saw lights in Cliff Castle!"

"Gosh!" said Peter, jumping out of bed and going to the window. "Did you really? I say — let's wake Brock."

But Brock was already awake, disturbed by the

noise. He was soon told what the matter was, and went to the window, too. All three watched for a little time – and then, suddenly, a light flickered again, this time at the bottom of the castle.

"There it is!" said Pam, clutching Peter and making him jump almost out of his skin. "Did you see it?"

"Of course," said Peter. "And there it is again – the first floor somewhere this time . . . and there again, higher up . . . and now it's right at the very top. Somewhere in that tower, look. It's the very tower we were in the other day!"

Pam felt a bit frightened. Who could be in the castle so late at night? The children watched for a little longer and then went back to bed, puzzled and excited.

"I vote we go there tomorrow again, and see if there's anyone there," said Brock. Nothing ever frightened Brock, and nothing ever stopped him from smiling! He meant to find out the secret of Cliff Castle as soon as possible!

So the next day three excited children met in Brock's playhouse in the garden to discuss their plans. They all felt certain that somebody was living in, or visiting, the castle – someone who had no right to be there. Who could it be – and why did he go there?

"When can we go?" asked Peter eagerly.

"After lunch," said Brock. "We're going over to the market this morning, in the next town. We don't want to miss that. It's fun. Dad will take us in his car."

So it was not until after the three children had been to the market, and had come back and eaten a most enormous lunch, that they set off to Cliff Castle once again.

They stopped at the little shop where once before they had bought lemonade. The woman served them again with fizzy drinks, which they drank in the shop.

"Any more been heard about the lights in Cliff Castle?" they asked the woman, when they paid her. She shook her head.

"Not that I know of," she said. "But don't you go wandering about there, my dears. It's a dangerous place."

They went off again, and soon came near the castle, which towered above them on its hill. They climbed the hill by the narrow rocky path and came to the big flight of overgrown stone steps.

"We won't go up the steps, in case there really is somebody in the castle, watching," said Peter. "We'll try and find that tiny little door. You know – the one we left latched."

So they made their way around nettle patches and other weeds until they came to where the little low door was set in the thick stone walls. The branches they had pulled from the nearby hedge were still against it. Nobody had disturbed them.

They pulled at the door, lifting the iron latch as they did so. It opened silently, and the children squeezed through, shutting it after them. They stood in the big kitchen, so dark and musty, shining their torches all around.

There was nothing new to be seen. They crossed the kitchen and went out into the hall – and here Brock gave a cry of surprise, and levelled his torch steadily on something on the ground.

The others looked. Pam couldn't make out why Brock was so excited, because all she saw were footprints crossing and recrossing the floor – and, after all, they had all walked there themselves last time!

"What's the matter?" she said.

"Can't you see, silly?" said Peter, pointing to a set of footprints that went across the floor. "Look at those. Those are not our marks. None of us have feet as big as that, and certainly we don't wear boots studded with nails. You can see the mark the nails have made in the thick dust."

Pam and the others stared at the marks. Yes – it

was quite plain that somebody grown-up had walked across that floor. Brock found another track and shone his torch on it.

"Two men have been here," he said thoughtfully. "Look – this set of prints shows a narrower foot than the other. Now, I wonder whatever two men were doing here?"

The children stared at one another. They couldn't imagine why men should visit the castle in the middle of the night. Perhaps they had come to steal something.

"Let's look in the rooms down here and see if anything has been disturbed," said Brock, at last. So they opened the nearest door and looked into the room there, still festooned with cobwebs, and still smelling of the same horrid, musty smell.

"Nothing has been moved," said Brock. "And there are only our footprints here. No one else's. Let's follow these other prints and see where they go. They show very clearly, don't they?"

They did show clearly in the thick dust. It was fairly easy to sort them out from the tracks the children themselves had made, for the men's prints were large and had made more impression in the dust. The children followed the prints up the big stairway to the first floor. There, neatly outlined in the dust, was something else!

"Look at that big oblong shape marked in the dust!" said Brock. "It looks as if someone had put down a big box there, doesn't it?"

"Yes," said Peter. "And look – there's the mark of another box, or something, further along. It looks as if the men had been carrying something very heavy up the stairs, and had put their load down for a rest before going on. See how their footprints are muddled here, too, as if they had picked up their load again and gone on carrying it further along."

"I feel rather like a detective!" said Pam excitedly. "Tracking things like this! I wonder where the men took their load to! I expect that explains the lights we saw last night. The men had torches, and every time they passed one of those slit-like windows, the reflection shone out for a moment, like a flicker. I guess they didn't know that!"

"Come on," said Brock impatiently. "Let's follow on."

They went on, past many closed doors and up another flight of stone steps. This brought them to the second floor. The footprints still went on!

"I believe they're going up to that tower!" said Pam. "We saw the light flicker there, you know. Oh – I hope the men aren't hiding there!"

This made the boys stop hurriedly. They hadn't thought of that! Suppose somebody was up there in the tower? That wouldn't be very pleasant, because they would be sure to be angry to see children interfering.

"We'd better go very quietly indeed, and not speak a word!" said Brock in a whisper. "Come on."

So in complete silence, their hearts beating fast, the three children crept on and up until they came to the room where the little stone staircase led up into the tower. They mounted it quietly, seeing the men's footprints still on the steps.

They came to the wooden door that had been open the first time they had gone up the staircase. This time it was shut!

6

A Puzzle

"It's shut!" whispered Brock. "Shall I try and open it?"

"No!" said Pam.

"Yes!" said Peter. Pam clutched Peter's hand. She didn't know what she expected to find behind that closed door, but she felt certain it wouldn't be nice! The boys felt that they really must push the door open. They were bursting with curiosity. Brock pushed. It didn't open. He took hold of the iron handle and tried to turn it. It turned — but still the door didn't open.

"Look through the keyhole and see if you can see anything," said Peter eagerly. "It's so big that maybe you can."

Brock put his eye to the keyhole. "It's all so dark," he said, "but I believe I can make out shapes of boxes and things. You take a peep, Peter."

So first Peter and then Pam peered through the keyhole, and they both agreed that certainly there were things there that hadn't been there before. They couldn't possibly see if they were boxes or trunks, or what they were, but there were things hidden there.

"If only we could get inside and see what's there!" said Brock longingly. "Something that ought not to be there, I'm sure!"

The castle was so silent and lonely, and the sound of their whispering voices was so peculiar, echoing down the stone stairway, that Pam felt nervous again. She pulled at Peter's arm.

"Let's go," she said. "We'll come back another time. Shall we tell anyone about what we know?"

"I don't think so," said Brock. "It's our own mystery. We've discovered it. Let's try and solve it ourselves. We often read about secrets and mysteries in books – it would be fun to try and keep this one all to ourselves."

They went downstairs again, puzzled to know what was in the tower, and why it was locked. When they got into the hall, Brock shone his torch towards the front door.

"I suppose the men came in at the front," he began – and then, he suddenly stopped. "Look!" he said. "There are no footsteps leading from the front door. Isn't that strange? How did the men get in, then?"

The three children stared in silence at the enormous door. Certainly the men had not used it.

Then which door had they used? As far as the children knew there was only one other door, and that was the little low one they themselves had used. They felt quite certain that the men had not used the window above, where the tree touched, because it was as much as the three children could do to squeeze inside there. No grown-up could possibly manage it.

"Let's follow all the footprints and see where they lead from," said Brock. "If we follow them all, we are sure to come to where the men entered."

So, their torches directed on the ground, the children followed the tracks patiently, one after

another. They couldn't understand one lot of tracks at all. They apparently led to, and came from, a room that had once been used as a study. The footprints went in and out of the door – there was a double-track, one going and one coming – and led across the room to the big fireplace, and back again.

"Why did the men come into this room, and go out again?" said Pam, puzzled. "They don't seem to have touched anything here. Why did they come here?"

"Goodness knows," said Brock, switching off his torch. "Just idle curiosity, or something, I suppose. There doesn't seem anything for them to come for here. I say – look at the time. We shall be awfully late for tea!"

"We'd better go, then," said Peter, who, although he wanted his tea, didn't want to leave the mystery unsolved like that. "Come on. We'll come back again soon."

They went into the kitchen and out of the little low door. They pushed it to behind them and piled the boughs against it, dragging the gorse bush round again. It hid the door well.

"I hope the men aren't as smart as we are!" said Brock, looking back at the castle. "We've left plenty of footprints there for them to see. They could easily tell that three children have been wandering about."

"I only wish I knew how the men got in and went out," said Peter, still worrying about that. "I feel sure there must be something in that room we last went into to account for their coming and going."

But it wasn't until late that night, when Peter was in bed, that he suddenly thought of something most exciting! Why ever hadn't he thought of it before? He sat up in bed and called Brock's name in such an urgent voice that Brock, half asleep, woke up in a hurry.

"What's up?" he said. "More lights showing in Cliff Castle?"

"No," said Peter. "But I believe I know how the men got in and out, Brock!"

"You don't!" said Brock.

"Well, listen – you know that often there were secret ways made into and behind rooms through the big chimneys they had in the old days," said Peter. "Well, I believe there must be some kind of way into that room – and that's how the men got into the castle!"

"Crumbs!" said Brock, wide awake now. "I never thought of that. I wonder if you're right. Maybe there's a secret entrance, then!"

"We'll go tomorrow and find out," said Peter, "even if we all get as black as sweeps exploring that chimney! We'll have a real adventure tomorrow!"

The two boys told Pam their idea in the morning, and the girl's eyes shone as she listened.

"Gracious! Do you really think there might be a secret way in and out of the castle through that big chimney-place? It's certainly enormous. I looked up it and it would take two or three men easily!"

To their disappointment the children could not go that day to the castle, because Brock's mother had planned a picnic for them. She was surprised when the three children did not seem pleased about it.

Next day the three children set off once more to the castle. They knew the way very well now and took a few short cuts so that it did not take them very long to arrive at the bottom of the hill. They stared up at the great castle, and it seemed to look down on them with a frown.

"Frown all you like!" said Brock, with a grin. "We'll find out your secret one day!"

They made their way to the little low door they knew and pulled it open. Into the vast kitchen they went, quite silently. Brock switched on his torch to see if there were any more footsteps to be seen. But there were none. In the hall and up the stairs were the same sets of prints that had been there before – there were no new ones, so far as the children could see.

"The men haven't been here again," said Brock. "Come on – let's go into that room where the prints led to and from the fireplace."

So into it they went, and followed the sets of prints to the big, open chimney-place. This was of stone, and the three children could easily stand upright in it!

"Now, we'll just have a hunt and see if, by any chance, there's a way out of the chimney itself," said Brock, and he switched his torch on to examine the stonework.

"Look!" cried Pam, pointing to something that ran up one side of the stone chimney. "A little iron ladder!"

The three of them stared at the little ladder. In the middle of each rung the rust had been worn away a little. "That's where the men went up and down!" cried Brock. "Come on – up we go! We're on to something here!"

7

A Strange Passage

Brock went first up the little iron ladder. Peter followed, and then Pam. The ladder went up some way, and then ended.

"It's come to an end!" cried Brock. "But there's a broad ledge here. I'll give you a hand up, Peter."

He pulled Peter up on to the stone ledge, and then the two boys pulled Pam up beside them. The ledge was broad enough to hold all the children quite comfortably.

"This funny ledge seems to have been made about halfway up the chimney, just before it begins to get very narrow," said Brock, pointing his torch upwards and showing the others how the chimney suddenly narrowed just above their heads. "We couldn't have gone up much further, even if there had been a ladder."

"Well, what did the men do?" said Pam, puzzled. "Surely they didn't just come to this ledge and go back?"

"Of course not!" said Brock. "This is where we use our brains a bit. Somewhere round about this ledge is the key to the secret passage that the men used. We've got to find it!"

"You don't mean a real key that turns, do you?" asked Pam, looking round and about with her torch, as if she expected to see a large iron key somewhere.

"Of course not," said Brock impatiently. "I don't exactly know what we're looking for, Pam – maybe a lever or a handle of some sort, or a stone that moves when it's pushed. We just don't know till we try."

So they tried. They hunted for any small bit of iron that might serve as a handle to move a stone. But they could find nothing in the walls around. They pushed against every stone they could reach, but they all seemed as solid as could be. They knocked with their knuckles to see if any stone sounded hollower than the rest, but except for taking the skin off their knuckles, there was no other result!

It was terribly disappointing. The children looked at one another after about twenty minutes, and wondered what else to do.

"I'm afraid we're beaten," said Peter, at last. "There doesn't seem a thing here that might show us where a secret passage is."

"There's only one place we haven't looked," said

Pam, suddenly. The boys stared at her.

"We've looked simply everywhere!" said Brock. "You know we have, silly."

"Well, we haven't looked at the stones we're standing on!" said Pam. "We've looked at the stonework round and above us – but not beneath our feet!"

"Pam's right!" said Brock excitedly. "Good for you, Pam. You certainly get the right ideas sometimes!"

Pam felt pleased. She only hoped she was right in her idea! The three of them knelt down to examine the stonework under their feet.

It wasn't long before Peter gave a loud cry, which made the others jump. "Look! What's this in this stone?"

They all looked closely, shining their torches down. Set deep in a hole in the rough stone was a sunken iron handle. On the stone by the handle a rough arrow was carved, pointing towards the chimney hole.

"This is it!" cried Peter. "Brock, what do we do? Pull at the handle?"

"Wait," said Brock. "This arrow means something. See where it points to? Well, I think we have to pull in that direction. Get off the stone, Pam, and Peter and I will see what we can do."

Pam took her foot off the stone, and watched as the two boys took hold of the iron handle and heaved at it in the direction of the arrow. At first nothing happened at all – and then a very strange thing came to pass under their eyes!

As the boys heaved at the handle, the stone in which it was set began to move smoothly outwards as if it were on rollers! It moved towards the chimney hole and then, when it seemed as if it really must overbalance and fall down the chimney, it stopped moving. In the space where it had been was a dark hole that led downwards!

"Look – there's something just a little way down, coiled up on a big staple!" cried Peter, and

he shone his torch on it. "It's a rope!"

Brock reached down and pulled it up. It wasn't a rope – it was a rope-ladder. He saw that the top of it was firmly hitched to the staple, and the rest dropped down out of sight. He let go and the rope ladder swung back to its staple.

"Well, that's the way we go!" said Brock. He shone his torch on to Pam. "What do you feel about it?" he asked. "I know girls aren't so daring as boys. Would you like Peter to take you outside and leave you to wait in the sunshine somewhere, while we see where this goes to? It might be a bit dangerous."

"Brock, don't be so mean!" cried Pam indignantly. "I'm not a coward – and do you suppose I want to go away from here just when things are getting really thrilling? I'm coming with you, so that's that."

"Righto," said Brock, grinning. "I thought you would. Don't get all hot and bothered about it. I'll go first. Peter, shine your torch down, old man."

Peter shone his torch down the curious hole, and Brock let himself over the edge and felt about with his feet for the first rung of the rope-ladder. Then down he went, very cautiously. After a bit, he shouted up: "The ladder has come to an end. There's a stone floor here, and a passage leading off. Come on down. Send Pam first, Peter, then you can give her a hand down."

So Pam went next, so excited that she could hardly feel for the rungs with her feet! She went down and down, and at last stood beside Brock, her feet safely on solid floor again. Then came Peter. They shone their torches into the passage that led off to the left of the strange hole.

"This is a real secret passage," said Brock in an excited voice. "A really proper one. Goodness – isn't it fun!"

"Come on," said Peter. "Let's see where it leads to. I can hardly hold my torch still, my hand is shaking so!"

They went down the narrow winding stone passage. It was perfectly dry, rather airless, and very small. In places the children had to bend their heads so as not to knock them against the roof of the passage.

The passage went steeply down, then at intervals turned right back on itself. "It must be made in the walls of the castle itself," said Brock wonderingly. "What a funny thing for anyone to have thought of making. Hello – what's this?"

A shaft of daylight had suddenly appeared in one side of the passage! It came from an iron grille set in the wall of the passage itself.

"A sort of air-hole, I suppose," said Peter, and he looked out. "I say, do you know where we are? We are at the west side of the castle – the side that goes sheer down with the steep cliff. I believe there must be a way cut down through the cliff itself, and the entrance to it is somewhere at the bottom of it!"

"Yes – you're right," said Brock, peering out too. "Well, if that's so, the passage will soon change from a stone one to an earth one – and let's hope it hasn't fallen in anywhere."

"Well, the men used it, didn't they?" said Peter.

Just as Brock said, the passage soon changed from a stone-walled one to one whose walls were made of earth, strengthened here and there by wood and stones. It zigzagged down, and at the steepest places steps were cut. It was not an easy way to take.

"We must surely be nearly at the bottom!" said Brock, at last. "My legs are getting jolly tired."

There was still a little way to go and then the secret passage ended abruptly in a small, low cave. The children crept into it, and then out into a larger cave. The entrance to this was set so closely about with gorse and blackberry bushes that it would have been quite impossible to see from the outside. The children forced their way out, tearing their clothes and scratching their legs.

"You can see where the men got in and out," said Brock. "Just there, where sprays of bramble are broken."

They looked round and about. They were now at the very bottom of the steep side of the cliff, where few people came. It was quite impossible to see the cave from where they stood, although they were only a few metres from it.

"Do you think we'd better climb back and swing that moving stone back into its place," Peter said suddenly. "If the men come again, as it's pretty certain they will, they'll see that stone is moved and suspect someone has been after them."

Brock looked at his watch. "We haven't time to do it," he said in dismay. "Gosh, Mum will be angry with us – it's half an hour past lunch-time already!"

"But, Brock, suppose the men see the stone has been moved?" said Peter anxiously.

"We'll come back another time and put it into its place," said Brock. "Maybe the men won't be back for some time now. They don't come every night. Come on, now – we'll have to race back!"

And race back they did but it didn't prevent them from being well scolded by Brock's mother!

8

Brock's Adventure

The children went to Brock's playhouse that afternoon and talked and talked about their discoveries in the castle. They couldn't say enough about the finding of the strange secret passage. When they remembered that long dark climb downwards through the walls of the castle, and then down the cliff itself, they felt more and more thrilled.

But Peter also went on feeling uncomfortable about the stone in the chimney. He kept saying that the men might come back and discover it.

"Perhaps you're right," said Brock, at last. "I'll slip off this evening after tea, by myself, and put it back. It won't take me long now I know all the short cuts."

"All right," said Peter. But it was not to be, for Brock's mother wanted him to drive the pony-cart over to the farm and collect a crate of chickens.

"Oh, Mum! Won't it do tomorrow?" said Brock in dismay. "I've got something I want to do."

"Well, I'm afraid that must keep till tomorrow,"

said his mother. "I've arranged with the farmer to send over for the chickens this evening and he'll have them all ready. Take Peter and Pam with you. It's a nice drive."

So Brock had to go off with his cousins in the pony-cart. "Just after I'd really made up my mind to go and do that at the castle," he grumbled. "I hate changing my plans. I really do feel you're right about that stone now, Peter."

"So do I," said Peter gloomily. "It would be just our luck if the men came tonight!"

"I'll tell you what I'll do!" said Brock, suddenly. "I'll go as soon as we're in bed! It will just be getting dark then, but the moon will be up early tonight, and I'll be able to see my way back beautifully."

"Oooh, Brock! You surely don't want to go to the castle at night-time!" cried Pam in horror. She felt quite nervous enough in the daytime, and she knew she would never be brave enough to go at night!

"Why not?" said Brock with a laugh. "You don't think I'm frightened, surely? It would take more than Cliff Castle to make me afraid!"

"Shall I come with you?" said Peter. He didn't really want to, but he felt he ought to make the offer.

"No thanks," said Brock. "I think it would be best for just one of us to go."

All Brock's family were early bedders, and it was about half past ten when the boy got cautiously out of bed and began to dress himself. Twilight still hung about the fields, but would soon disappear. Then the moon would come up.

"Good luck, Brock!" whispered Peter. "Do you think your father and mother are asleep?"

"I don't know," said Brock. "I'm not going to risk going downstairs and opening any of the doors. They're sure to creak!"

"Well, how are you going, then?" asked Peter in astonishment.

"Down my old apple tree!" whispered Brock, and Peter saw the flash of his white teeth as he grinned.

He went to the window and put a leg across. He caught hold of a strong branch and in a moment had worked his way down it to the trunk. Then down he slid and Peter heard the soft thud of his feet on the ground below. He watched the boy's shadowy figure as he ran down the garden and out into the lane.

"I hope he won't be too long," thought Peter, as he curled up in bed again. "I shall keep awake till he comes back. Then I'll pop up and wake Pam, and she can come down and hear what Brock has to say."

But Peter didn't keep awake. By the time that half past eleven had struck downstairs, he was fast asleep!

But Brock was wide awake, running like a hare over the fields. He met nobody, for no one was out so late at night in the country. Grazing sheep lifted their heads to look at him and a startled rabbit skipped out of his way.

Brock saw the moon coming up slowly. It lit up the castle on the hill, and made it look silvery and unreal.

"It's like a castle out of some old story," thought the boy. "It will be fun to get inside at night-time!"

Brock was quite fearless. He enjoyed this kind of adventure and was quite glad to be on his own without the others to bother about. He ran round to where the little low door was set at the bottom of the castle. He pulled at it and it opened.

He slipped inside. He waited a moment in the great dark kitchen to see if anyone else was about by any chance, but everything was still and silent. The boy switched his torch on and went into the hall to see if there were any more footprints. But there were none. So the men hadn't yet been – but, after all, it wasn't many hours since Brock had left, and it didn't leave much time for anyone to come.

The boy made his way to the room where the iron ladder led up the chimney. He climbed up the ladder and soon came to the ledge. The stone that had moved out to disclose the secret passage was still swung out over the chimney hole. Brock wondered how to get it back.

"I suppose I must heave on the iron handle in the opposite direction," he thought. He took hold of it, and then almost fell down the hole in astonishment. He had heard voices!

"Gosh!" thought the boy, sitting quite still on the ledge, "somebody is coming – two people at least. But where do the voices come from?"

Brock couldn't distinguish any words, he could only hear the murmur of voices talking and answering. They came up from the hole, and were getting louder.

"My goodness, someone is coming up through the secret passage!" thought the boy, in a fright for the moment. "It must be those men. I must get the stone back into place as quickly as I can!"

With the sound of voices came other sounds, rather like something being bumped against the wall. Brock felt sure the men were carrying something again. He took hold of the iron handle sunk in the stone and heaved hard at it. At first the stone would not move, then, slowly and gradually, it gave way to Brock's stout pulling and rolled back into its place.

It made a slight grinding noise as it did so, and Brock hoped that the men below were talking loudly enough to drown the sound. He climbed quickly down the iron ladder and ran into the kitchen, meaning to get out of the little low door.

Then he stopped. "No," he said to himself. "This is a big chance for me to find out exactly what the men are up to. I'll hide somewhere, and listen and follow. Goodness, what an adventure!"

He darted behind a big cupboard in the hall and waited to see what happened. After some while he heard sounds coming from the room he had left. The men were climbing down the iron ladder in the chimney-place, dragging something heavy with them.

Then came the sound of voices, quite clearly echoing weirdly through the silent castle.

"We ought to be paid double for bringing the goods up that narrow way!" grumbled one voice. "I'd be willing to risk the front door, but Galli won't hear of it. Come on – we've got to take the things up to the tower now. Then we'll get away quickly. I don't like this wretched moon, showing us up so clearly when we walk outside."

From his hiding-place Brock could see two men, each carrying large and heavy boxes on their backs. They were half-bent beneath the weight, and the boy marvelled that they could possibly have carried them all the way up the secret passage, up the rope-ladder, and then down the iron one!

"They must be very strong," thought the boy. They were. They had broad shoulders, and when they were caught in a shaft of bright moonlight, Brock saw that they looked rather foreign. He had thought that their voices sounded a little foreign too. One man wore gold earrings in his ears.

They came into the hall, carrying the boxes, and then went up the broad flight of stairs. They put the boxes down for a rest when they came to the top, and again Brock heard the murmur of their voices as they spoke together. The boy crept out from his hiding-place and went to the foot of the stairs.

He followed the men silently up and up until they went into the room from which the little stone staircase led into the tower room. One of the men unlocked the door at the top. Brock heard them put down their loads and sigh with relief.

"I could do with a drink now," said one man. "Is there a tap in the kitchen – or somewhere we can get water?"

"We'll look," said the other. He locked the door, and the men came down the narrow staircase again. Brock saw that they had left the key in the door and his eyes gleamed. Maybe he could slip up and take it out before they remembered it – and then he and the others could come and find out what was in those boxes! Something exciting, he was sure!

He slipped out before the men and ran into one of the nearby rooms. It was furnished, and the boy pulled some curtains round him to hide himself. But the things were quite rotten and fell away as he touched them. Thin grey dust flew all round, and before Brock could stop himself, he sneezed!

9

Brock in Trouble

Now when Brock sneezed, everyone knew it, for he sneezed heartily and well. In the silence of the castle his sneeze made a most tremendous noise! It echoed all round and about, and startled poor Brock just as much as it startled the two men.

"There's someone here!" said one. "In that room. Quick – we'll get him!"

They darted into the room where Brock had tried to hide. Luckily for him they missed him and he was able to dart out and elude their outstretched hands. He ran down the stairs at top speed, his feet making a tremendous clatter as he went.

The men ran after him. Down and down went Brock, meaning to make for the little low door in the kitchen. But when he got there, it was so dark he could not see where he was going and he fell over a stool. He crashed to the floor and had no time to make for the door. Instead, he rolled quickly under a big oak seat in the fireplace and lay there, hardly daring to breathe. The men switched on their torches, and one of them exclaimed:

"Look – here's a little door, ajar!"

"That's where the boy came in!" said the other man. "Well, he didn't have time to get out, that's certain. He's somewhere here. But first I think we'll shut and lock the door. Then our friend won't be able to escape quite so easily as he hoped!"

Poor Brock heard the door being shut and locked. He felt certain that the man had put the key in his pocket. He couldn't think what to do. He wondered if the men knew of the little back staircase. If he could run up that he might be able to find the room where the big tree touched the windowsill. Then he'd be out in a jiffy and the men couldn't follow him!

"Let's shut the kitchen door and have a good hunt round," said one man. "He's here somewhere."

Now was Brock's chance. The big kitchen door was at the far end of the kitchen. He stood up quietly and then made a dash for the little back staircase, which was quite near by. The men gave a shout when they heard him and moved their torch-beams round to the noise.

"There's a stairway there!" cried one. "He's gone up. Come on – after him!"

The men tore up the narrow stairway after

Brock. "If only I could remember which room that tree touched!" thought the boy desperately. "But we couldn't find it again before. There are so many rooms here, all exactly the same!"

He ran on till he came to a room and then he darted inside. He took off his boots quickly because he knew that the noise they made gave him away and made him easy to follow.

The men passed the room, flashing their torches ahead of them. Brock ran to the window. Alas, it was not the right one. It was far too narrow to squeeze through.

Brock ran to the door and peered out. The men had gone to the other end of the stone landing and were looking into each of the rooms as they came back. Brock ran into the one next to his. Again he was disappointed. It was not the right one. He went into a third, his heart beating fast, for the men were now coming back. But again he was unlucky.

He did not dare to go into another room. The only thing he could do was to run back to the staircase and go down it, hoping to hide himself so well somewhere that he would not be found.

As he ran to the staircase the men saw him in a shaft of moonlight and raced after him. Brock almost fell down the stairs, and raced across the kitchen into the hall. Then he tore into one of the big, furnished rooms, meaning to hide behind some furniture.

The men saw him. They went into the room after him, and in a few moments they had found Brock and dragged him out from behind a big dusty couch that smelled so mouldy that the boy was almost sick.

"Well, we've got you now!" said the man. He shone his torch into Brock's face. "What are you doing here, spying on us? You're doing a

dangerous thing. We can't let you go, because you've found our secret and we daren't risk your telling it till we've finished our job and are safe."

Brock said nothing. His round face looked surly. The men looked at one another.

"What are we to do with him?" said one. "He's only a kid. We'd better lock him up somewhere and tell Galli. Then he can put him away till it's safe to let him go. Well, youngster, you'll be sorry for yourself when Galli gets hold of you. He won't be gentle with a nasty little boy who spies on him!"

Still Brock said nothing. One of the men gave him a shake. "He's lost his tongue," he said to the other. "Come on – let's lock him up in the tower room with the boxes. He'll be safe there."

So Brock was dragged up to the tower room, and put there among the big boxes. The men locked the door behind them, and Brock heard their footsteps going down the stairs. He felt sure they would go out by the little low door instead of the difficult way down the secret passage. And they would lock the door behind them, so that Peter and Pam couldn't get in if they came to look for him.

"I've made a mess of things," said Brock, looking at the big boxes. "I wonder what's in those boxes. How I'd like to know!"

He shone his torch on to one, but soon saw that

it was so well fastened and nailed down that it would need strong tools to open it. His bare hands and pocket-knife would be no good at all! He went to a window and looked out gloomily on the countryside. A ray of moonlight came through the slit. Far away, Brock could see his own house.

As he looked at it, he saw a light moving in one of the windows. He tried to reckon out which it was, and soon came to the conclusion that it was his own window. Then Peter must be awake. That must have been his torch shining!

In a second Brock took out his own torch again, and pushed it as far as he could through the slit. He pressed the knob of the torch up and down, so that it flashed regularly and continually.

"If only Peter sees it, he may guess it's me," thought the boy. "Oh, I do hope he sees it! I don't want to be kept a prisoner here for days!"

10

Peter and Pam to the Rescue!

Peter slept soundly till half past one. Then he woke up with a jump. He remembered at once that Brock had gone to Cliff Castle, and he sat up in bed to see if the boy was back.

He stared at Brock's empty bed, and then switched on his torch to look at his watch. Half past one! Whatever could Brock be doing?

As he sat wondering, he heard a sound at the door, and almost jumped out of his skin as a white figure came into the room. It was Pam in her nightdress.

"Peter! Is Brock back? You said you'd come up and wake me when he came back, but it's awfully late."

Peter shone his torch on to Brock's empty bed. Pam felt scared.

"Goodness! Where is he?" She went to the window and stared out at the big black mass of Cliff Castle. The moon had gone in for a moment, and it looked very dark and forbidding. Then she suddenly caught sight of a bright little light winking and blinking in the top tower to the right.

"That's funny," she said to Peter. "Look at that light, flashing every other moment, Peter, just as if it were a signal. Those men wouldn't do that, would they, because they wouldn't want to give themselves away. But who else would be signalling like that?"

Peter looked, and as soon as he saw the winking light he guessed that it was Brock. "It's Brock!" he said. "I'm quite sure it is! What's he doing in the tower room – it was locked, wasn't it? He must have got in somehow and wants us to go and see what the treasure is in those boxes!"

"Or do you think he's been captured?" said Pam slowly. "He might have been, you know. Maybe he's locked up in the tower."

"We'd better go and see," said Peter, beginning to dress hurriedly. "We won't tell Aunt Hetty, or Uncle, Pam, in case Brock wants us to go and see the treasure with him without anyone knowing. We don't want to give the secret away unless we have to! Hurry and dress now!"

It wasn't long before the two children were climbing down the old apple tree and sliding to the ground below. Then they made their way to Cliff Castle, panting as they ran.

They got there safely and went to where the

little low door was set in the kitchen wall. Peter pulled at it, expecting it to open. But it didn't. It remained tightly shut.

"I say! It's locked or something!" he said to Pam. "Here, help me to pull."

But pulling was no use at all. The little wooden door wouldn't budge!

"Well, Brock wouldn't have locked it, that's certain," said Peter, speaking in a whisper. "Someone else must have. I say — I rather think Brock's been captured!"

"How shall we get in, then?" Pam whispered. "Up that tree? But, Peter, surely we can't climb it in the dark."

"We'll have to try," said Peter. "Look, the moon will be out for some time now — we'll climb while it gives us a bright light. I'll help you. Or would you rather stay on the ground while I climb?"

"No, I'll climb, too," said Pam bravely. So they made their way to the tree and Peter shinned up it first. But Pam couldn't climb it because her legs trembled so. "I'll just have to stay here," she whispered up to him. "I shall fall if I climb up, Peter. Isn't it sickening?"

"Never mind, old girl," said Peter. "You stay down below and warn me if anyone comes. I'll go in and see if I can rescue Brock."

Pam couldn't see Peter climbing the tree because it was full of dark shadows, flecked by moonlight. She heard the rustling, though, and knew when Peter had reached the bough that led to the window because of the sudden swinging of the tree.

Peter didn't find it so easy to climb the tree in the dark as in the light, but he managed to slide down the branch to the window, and then squeezed himself through. He jumped down to the floor and ran on tiptoe to the door, not making a sound. When he got there he looked out and suddenly remembered how hard it had been to find that room again. With the toe of one of his boots he made a big cross in the dust of the floor. Now he had only to pop his head in at the door to see the cross and know it was the room with the tree outside.

"I feel quite clever!" said the boy to himself. He ran to the little stone staircase and went lightly down it. The moon was now high and shone in at every slit-like window, so that it was fairly easy to see, though the shadows were as black as could be.

Across the kitchen went the boy, and into the dark hall. Then up the broad flight of stairs on the other side and on to the first landing. He paused there in the shadows to listen. Was there anyone about? After all, if Brock had been captured, someone must have captured him and it was quite likely they might still be somewhere in the castle. This was rather a weird thought, and the boy felt a shiver down his back.

"I won't get frightened!" he thought to himself. "I'm rescuing Brock, and I'm not afraid of anything."

He would have liked to whistle to keep his spirits up, but he didn't dare to. As it was, every little sound he made went echoing round and round and made him jump.

He went on up to the floor where the room was that had the tower staircase leading from it. He came to the stairway and stood at the bottom, his heart beating so loudly that he felt sure anyone nearby could hear it!

He stole up the staircase and felt the shut door. He longed to push it open, but he still didn't know if Brock was behind it, or an enemy. And then, suddenly, he knew!

There came the sound of a sigh, and then a creak as if someone had sat down on a box. "Blow my torch!" said a gloomy voice. "It's no use now – the battery's given out. I can't signal any more."

It was Brock's voice. In delight Peter banged on the door, making poor Brock inside almost jump out of his skin, for he had, of course, no idea at all that Peter was anywhere near. He almost fell off the box.

"Brock!" came Peter's voice. "I'm here. I'm coming. What's happened?" Peter pushed at the door – but alas, it was locked, and wouldn't open. Brock's voice came in excitement from behind the door:

"Peter! You old brick! Is the key in the lock?"

"No," said Peter, switching on his torch. "What a blow! I can't get in – and you can't get out."

Brock told him shortly how he had been captured. "And now I'm sitting on a box that may contain half the jewels in the kingdom!" he said. "But I'm a prisoner, and likely to remain one till this man Galli they keep talking about comes along and decides what's to be done with me."

"I'll go back home and get your father to come, and the police," said Peter eagerly. "I don't expect the men will be back tonight."

"Where's Pam?" said Brock. "Fast asleep in bed, I hope!"

"No. She's outside the castle, waiting," said Peter. "She couldn't climb the tree in the dark. She said she'd keep watch in case someone came."

"I say, Peter! I've got an idea!" said Brock suddenly. "Maybe the other towers have little rooms inside them, with a door like this one. And maybe they all have locks and keys that are the same. Do you think you could go to the tower on this side and see if there's a key in the door of the room there? If there is, bring it back and try it in this lock – it may fit and open the door!"

"Gosh! That's an idea!" cried Peter, and he went down the staircase and made his way round the big stone landing until he came to the end. He went into the room there and found a staircase leading up to the tower above, exactly like the one in the room he had left. Up he went and came to a door.

"And, my goodness, there is a key in the lock!" said the boy to himself, in delight. He pulled out the key and made his way back. He fitted it into the lock of Brock's door – and it turned! The lock gave and the door opened.

"Oh, Peter, what luck!" said Brock, and he squeezed his cousin's arm. "Thanks a million – you're marvellous to come and rescue me. Now we must go straight down and join Pam, and then I think we ought to rush home and wake up my father. Someone ought to come and see what's in these boxes!"

Down the little stone staircase went the two boys. They felt tremendously excited, and Peter's hand shook as he held out his torch to show the way. The mystery of Cliff Castle was nearly solved. The secret was in those boxes. Soon Brock's father would come along and open them. Then, maybe, the two men would be caught and everything would be cleared up.

Just as they reached the first landing they had a terrific shock. A great crashing echoed throughout the whole castle, and the two boys jumped so much that they had to stand still. What in the world could the noise be?

11

More and More Excitement

The enormous crash came again – and then the boys knew what it was!

"It's somebody banging on that great front door knocker!" cried Peter.

"But who would do that in the middle of the night?" said Brock, amazed.

"Pam, of course," said Peter proudly. "She said she'd watch out – and I expect she's seen someone coming and that's her way of warning us. What a marvellous idea!"

"I say, what a girl she is!" said Brock admiringly. "Well, we'll have to look out. Let's slip down to the kitchen and see if we can get out of that little low door. Maybe the key is on this side."

They ran quietly down the stairs, then paused in horror at the bottom. In the kitchen waiting silently, themselves amazed at the noise from the front door, were three men. Two of them Brock had seen before.

The men saw the boys and gave a shout. "Two kids this time!" cried one. "Quick, get them!"

The boys tore into the hall and into the big room where the chimney was that gave on to the secret passage. Brock slammed the door and turned the key in the lock. Then they rushed to the fireplace and climbed quickly up the iron ladder. A heave at the iron ring and the stone moved silently across, showing the way down.

A great noise at the locked door made the boys hurry more than ever. The door would certainly be down very soon, for the lock was sure to be rotten!

It was! It gave way and the door swung open. The three men rushed in and paused. "Surely those kids don't know the secret passage!" cried one of the men in amazement.

"They do!" said another. "Come on – we must get them, somehow, or they'll be away, and tell the police."

They rushed to the fireplace and swarmed up the iron ladder. By this time the boys were at the bottom of the rope ladder, making their way as quickly as they could down the secret stone passage, their hearts beating painfully. They could hear the men coming after them, and hurried more and more. They came to where the stone passage ended and the earth passage began.

"Hurry, Brock, hurry!" cried Peter. "They're almost on us. Hurry!"

The boys ran down the passage and at last came to the small cave and made their way into the larger one. Just as the men got to the small cave the boys forced their way out of the large one, and found themselves on the hillside.

"Up a tree, quick!" whispered Brock. "It's our only chance!"

Peter shinned up a nearby tree, with Brock helping him. Then Brock swung himself up into the dark shadows and both boys lay flat on branches, peering down below, hardly daring to breathe.

It didn't occur to the men that the boys could so quickly have gone up a tree. They thought they had run off into the bushes and they beat about quickly to find them.

"They'll give it up soon," whispered Brock. He was right. The men soon gave up the search and gathered together. The third man, called Galli, was very angry.

"Fancy letting a couple of kids beat you like this!" he said in disgust. "Now there's only one thing to do; get the stuff out of the tower room at once and find a new hiding-place. Go on – get back to the castle and haul the stuff out."

The men went off, the other two muttering angrily to themselves, but they were evidently terrified of Galli, who was the leader.

The men went back up the secret passage. As soon as they were safely out of hearing, the boys slid down the tree into the moonlight and looked at one another excitedly.

"Let's get back home as quickly as we can!" said Peter. "We'll fetch Pam, and run as fast as possible."

"The men will be gone by the time we get Dad and the police here," panted Brock, as they ran up the slope that led to the front of the castle to find Pam. She saw them coming and jumped out from under a bush.

"Brock! Peter! Oh, how glad I am to see you! Did you hear me crash on the knocker? I saw the three men coming and they went in at that little low door. I couldn't think how to warn you – and I suddenly thought of that great knocker!"

"Pam, you're a marvellous girl!" said Brock, and he threw his arm round his cousin's shoulders and gave her a hug. "Nobody but you would have thought of such an idea! Honestly, I'm proud of you!"

The boys quickly told Pam what had happened to them – and then Brock suddenly fell silent. The other two looked at him.

"What is it, Brock?" asked Peter.

"I've got an idea, but I don't know if it's good or

not," said Brock. "Listen. Those men are all going back to the tower room, aren't they? Well, do you suppose – do you possibly suppose we could get there, too, and wait till they're inside, and then lock them in?"

Peter and Pam stared at Brock. It seemed a mad idea – and yet – suppose, just suppose it could be done!

"The men would never, never guess we were back again," said Peter slowly. "They wouldn't be on the lookout for us. They think we're running off to tell the police. It seems to me that your idea is the only one that might possibly lead to the capture of the men – and the goods, too! Otherwise, by the time we get back here with help, they'll be gone with everything!"

"We'll try it!" said Brock. "Now, look here, Pam – your part in this is to race off by yourself over the fields and wake Dad and Mum, and tell them everything. Will you do that?"

Pam didn't at all want to do anything of the sort, but she wasn't going to let the boys down. She nodded her head. "I'll go," she said, and she went, running like a little black shadow down the hillside.

"She's a good kid," said Brock, and the two boys turned to go to the castle. They meant to climb up the tree and get in that way. They were sure the little low door would be locked. Up they went and into the dark room. There, on the floor, was the cross in the dust that Peter had made!

"Now, quietly!" whispered Brock, as they went down the narrow stone staircase. "The men may be in the kitchen, or the hall."

The boys stole carefully down. There was no one in the kitchen – and no one in the hall. The boys kept to the shadows as they walked.

Suddenly they heard a noise, and Peter clutched Brock by the arm, pulling him into the shadow of a great hall curtain. "It's the men coming out of the chimney-place," whispered the boy. "They're only just back. It's taken them ages to come up by that steep secret passage. Keep quiet now. We may be able to do something."

The men clattered across the room to the door and then went across the hall to the big staircase, talking in loud voices. It was quite clear that they had no idea at all that the boys were hidden nearby. They went up the stairs, and as soon as they had turned a corner, the boys followed them, so full of excitement that they could hardly breathe!

The three men went on up to the tower room. The boys could hear their voices all the time.

They crept after them, never having felt so

terribly excited in their lives!

All the men went into the tower room. Peter and Brock stood at the bottom of the little staircase that wound up to the room, and wondered if this was the right moment to go up.

"Better do it now," said Brock, "or they will start to come out again."

Galli, up above, gave orders to the two men. "Take that box first. And hurry up about it!"

There came the sounds of two men swinging a box round to get hold of it.

"Now!" whispered Brock, and the two boys shot up the stairs, one behind the other, breathing fast. They got to the door. The men hadn't heard a sound. By the light of their torches Brock could see two of them lifting one of the boxes, while Galli stood by. The boy caught hold of the wooden door, and closed it as quietly as he could. But it made a slight click as the latch went into place. At once Galli noticed it and roared out a warning.

"Look out! There's somebody on the stairs!" He rushed to the door, but Brock had already turned the key in the lock.

Galli hammered on the door in a rage and the stout door shook under his blows.

"You can hammer all you like!" shouted Brock exultingly. "You're caught!"

The boys turned to go down the stairs, and then Peter's sharp ears caught something that one of the men said.

"I've got a key to this door! I took it out of the lock when I shut up that kid. Here, take it, Galli, and undo the door. We'll catch those boys if we have to hunt the castle from top to bottom!"

Peter clutched Brock by the arm. "Did you hear that? They've got the key to this door, Brock! The one that was in the door when they locked you up! Now what are we to do?"

Brock dashed up the stairs again. He switched his torch on to the door, at the same moment as he heard a key being put into the lock from the other side. His torch showed him a big bolt at the top of the door and another at the bottom. Hoping and praying that they would not be too rusty to push into place, the boy took hold of the bottom bolt. He pulled at it, but it stuck badly.

Meantime the men on the other side of the door were trying to turn the key to unlock it. But it was more difficult to do that from inside than outside. Muttering a string of foreign-sounding words, Galli tried to force the key round.

"Let me try the bolt, Brock," whispered Peter, and took Brock's place. But it was no use. He could only move it a little way, it was so rusty.

"Try the top one," said Brock. So Peter stood on tiptoe and tried the one at the top. He was trembling from head to foot, for it was terrible to hear someone doing his best to unlock the door from the inside, while he, Peter, was trying with all his might to bolt it from the outside!

"Oh Peter, Peter, won't it move?" groaned Brock, feeling certain that they would be captured if the door was unlocked. Peter suddenly gave a shout, and there was a creaking sound. The rust on the bolt had given way and the bolt had slid slowly into place. The door was bolted!

Almost at the same moment the key turned on the other side and unlocked the door — but it was held by the bolt, and Galli roared with rage as he found that the door would not budge. It gave at the bottom, but the stout bolt at the top held firmly.

The boys were both shaking. They had to sit down on the stairs and lean against one another. Neither boy could have gone down the stairs at that moment. They sat there, close to each other, and heard the three men losing their tempers with one another. They shouted in a strange language, and at times one of them would shake the door with all his strength.

"I hope that top bolt holds," said Peter in a whisper. "Everything in this house is so rotten and old that I wouldn't be surprised if the wretched thing gives way."

"Well, let's try to use the bottom bolt as well then, when the men leave the door alone for a moment," whispered back Brock. "Come on – there's a chance now."

The boys, both together, tried to move the bottom bolt back into place. Peter took Brock's knife and scraped away the rust as best he could. Then they tried again – and to their great joy and relief, the bolt slowly and haltingly slipped into

place. Now the door was held at top and bottom, and the boys felt pretty certain that the men could not possibly get out, even if they tried all their strength together on the door.

The men did try once more – and this time they found, of course, that it would not move at the bottom.

"They've fastened the door at the bottom, too, now!" shouted Galli, and the angry man struck the door with his fists, and kicked at it viciously with his foot.

"Hope he hurts himself!" whispered Brock, who was feeling much better now. He had stopped shaking, and was grinning to himself to think how neatly all the men were boxed up together. "I say, Peter – I rather think we've done a good night's work!"

"I rather think we have, too!" said Peter, and the two boys hugged themselves as they thought of all they had gone through to catch the men.

"I hope Pam gets home safely," said Brock. "I wonder how long it will be before she brings help back. Some time, I expect, because Dad will have to get in touch with the police. Well – I'm quite content to wait here till somebody arrives. I guess we're feeling a bit more comfortable than those three men!"

12

The Secret Comes Out!

Meantime Pam was speeding across the fields and along the shadowy lanes. Once she had started she no longer felt afraid. She had to bring help to the boys, and that help rested on her swift feet. "Quick, quick!" she kept saying. "I must run like the wind!"

And run like the wind she did. She came to her aunt's house at last, and hammered on the front door, for she did not want to waste time by climbing in at the window. Her uncle awoke at once and came to his window. When he saw Pam standing there in the moonlight he thought he must be dreaming.

"Uncle! Uncle! Let me in, quick!" cried Pam. "There isn't a moment to be lost! The boys are in danger!"

In two minutes Pam was inside the house, sitting on her uncle's knee, pouring out the whole story to him as quickly as she could. He and his wife listened in the utmost amazement. Aunt Hetty could hardly believe the story, but Pam's uncle did at once, and saw that he must act quickly.

"I'll hear all the rest later," he said to the excited little girl. "If those two boys have managed to capture the men as they planned, we must go there at once – and if they haven't managed to, they'll be in the gravest danger. I'll ring up the police now. Hetty, see to Pam. She'd better go back to bed."

But nothing in the world would have persuaded Pam to go back to bed that night! "I'll climb out of the window if you make me go to bed!" she cried. "Oh, Aunt Hetty, I must go back to Cliff Castle. I must, I must!"

And, as it turned out, she did, because when her uncle came back from the telephone he said that the police wanted her to go with them to take them to the right room. It wasn't long before a police car roared up to the house with four tall policemen inside!

Pam and her uncle squeezed into the car too, and they set off to Cliff Castle by the road. It was a much longer way than across the fields, but it didn't take very long in the powerful police car.

"Why, look at that light in the sky!" said Pam suddenly, pointing to the east. "What is it, Uncle?"

"It's the dawn coming!" said her uncle, with a laugh. "The night is going. Hasn't it been a long enough night for you, Pam?"

"Yes, it has," said Pam, suddenly feeling glad that it would soon be daylight. "I wonder how we can get into the castle, Uncle? There are four ways in – but three of them are almost impossible."

"What are the four ways, Pam?" asked the inspector, who was sitting beside her.

"There's the front door," said Pam, "but the locks and bolts are all rusted and we couldn't open it. Then there's a little low door set in the foot of the castle by the kitchen – but that's shut and locked. And there's a secret passage from the bottom of the steep cliff, through the walls of the castle, and up a chimney."

"My word!" said the inspector, startled. "However did you find out all this? I must say you children are pretty daring! What's the fourth way in?"

"It's the way we used first," said Pam. "Up a tree and in at a window. But I'm afraid you're all too big to squeeze in there!"

"We'll break in at the little low door!" said the inspector with a chuckle. And that is exactly what they did do!

The two boys were still sitting together on the stairs, feeling rather sleepy, watching the dawn put silver fingers in at the slits of windows, when they suddenly heard the noise of the police car roaring up to the castle. Then they heard loud blows on the little door far below.

"They're breaking in!" cried Brock, in excitement, and he jumped to his feet, almost falling down the stairway. "They're knocking down that little door. Now they're in . . . gosh, they're here! Pam! Pam! Here we are!"

Pam came tearing up the big staircase, followed by her uncle and the four policemen. She rushed into the room off which the little winding stairway led up to the tower room, shouting as she came.

"Peter! Brock! Did you manage to catch the men? Uncle's here and four policemen!"

"Yes, we've got the men!" shouted Brock, and grinned as he saw Pam's excited face coming round the bend in the stairway. "We've bolted them in well and truly!"

The men had fallen silent when they heard the shouts. They knew perfectly well that everything was up as far as they were concerned.

"Get away down the stairs, you three children," commanded the inspector, his voice suddenly taking on a new and quite stern tone. The children badly wanted to be in at the finish but they didn't dare to say a word. They had to go and wait in the room below while the police unbolted the door and rushed at the three men.

There was a lot of yelling and struggling but the five men against the three were too strong, and it wasn't long before a sorry procession came down the winding stairway in the charge of three policemen.

"Take them into a room and stay with them till I come," ordered the inspector. Then he beckoned to the three children.

"Come along," he said, "we're going to open those boxes. You deserve to see what's inside, since it was you who really captured the men!"

In the greatest excitement, the children followed the inspector and Brock's father upstairs into the tower room. The great boxes lay there, still unopened.

The inspector had the right tools with him and began to force open the boxes quickly. They were very well fastened indeed, and even when the clasps had been forced back, the ropes cut, and the iron bands severed, there were still the locks to open. But the inspector had marvellous keys for these. "One of these keys will open the locks," he told the watching children. "It's my boast that I've got the keys to open any lock in the world!"

The locks of the first box clicked. The inspector threw back the heavy lid. What looked like cotton wool lay on the top. Pam pulled it aside. Then everyone cried out in astonishment and awe – for lying in the box were the most marvellous jewels that the children had ever seen or heard of. Great red rubies shone and glowed in necklaces and tiaras. Brilliant green emeralds winked, and diamonds blazed in the light of the torches that shone down on the jewels.

"I say!" said Brock's father, finding his tongue first. "I say – Inspector, these are not ordinary jewels. They are worth a fortune – many fortunes! What are they?"

"Well, it looks to me as if this is the private jewellery of the Princess of Larreeanah," said the inspector. "They were stolen when she fled from her palace in India to this country. It's an amazing story. She had them all put into these boxes and safely fastened in many ways. They were apparently guarded night and day – and were taken with her when she landed in this country. But when the boxes were opened at her bank in London, they contained nothing but stones!"

"But how could that be?" said Pam, her eyes opening wide in amazement. "And how are they here, then?"

"Well, I suppose what happened was that one of the guards was bribed by some clever thief who knew what was contained in the boxes," said the inspector. "He must have had boxes of exactly the same size and make all ready, filled with stones – probably hidden inside big trunks of his own. At the right moment he must have got into the place where these boxes were stored, exchanged them, and then put these boxes into his own trunks and got away safely with them."

"And the poor princess went off with the boxes of stones!" cried Brock. "Was it that man Galli, do you think?"

"Yes, I should think so," said the inspector, beginning to open another box. "He looks very like a famous thief, one of the cleverest we have ever come up against, whom we already want for another daring robbery. He's shaved off his moustache and beard, but I noticed that he had a little finger missing and so has the thief I was telling you about! My word – look at this!"

The second box was now open, and contained just as amazing treasures as the first. Pam took out a wonderful tiara, rather like a small crown, and put it on.

"Now you're worth about a hundred thousand pounds!" said her uncle. "Do you feel grand and important?"

"Oh, very!" said Pam, with a laugh.

"Well, you've every right to feel like that," said

the inspector, shutting the first box and locking it. "But not because you're wearing famous jewels. You can feel grand and important because you and your brother and cousin have made it possible for us to recover all this jewellery and to catch the thieves who stole it! At the moment I should say you are the most daring and clever children in the whole country!"

Even Brock blushed at this. All the children felt pleased.

"Well, it didn't seem very clever or daring while we were doing it," said Peter honestly. "As a matter of fact, I kept feeling frightened – and I know poor old Pam did."

"It's braver to do a thing if you feel afraid than it is to do it if you don't mind," said the inspector. "I don't know what to do with these boxes. I think I'll handcuff those three men together, send them off in charge of two of my men, and leave the third man here on guard while I go and report to Scotland Yard."

"What's Scotland Yard?" said Pam in surprise.

"It's the place where all the head policemen work!" said the inspector, with a sudden grin. "Very important place, too! Well – come along. You children must be tired out."

They went down the stairs. The inspector gave

his orders and the three sullen thieves were handcuffed together, so that two policemen could easily take charge of them. The third one was sent up to guard the tower room.

"I'll send back a car for Galli and the others," said the inspector. "I'll take these children home, and then their uncle can come along with me to the station."

Pam almost fell asleep in the car. She was completely tired out. But the two boys were still excited. They looked out of the car windows at the sun just rising in the eastern sky. It seemed ages and ages since yesterday! Could so much have possibly happened in one night?

Brock's mother made all the children go to bed when they got back. "You look absolutely worn out," she said. "Tell me everything when you wake, Pam. I'll undress you. You are falling asleep as you stand!"

The boys were glad to get into bed now, though it seemed odd to go to bed when the sun was just rising. Brock snuggled down.

"Well, goodnight," he said to Peter. "I mean, good morning! What adventures we've had. I'm sorry they're over. I did enjoy solving the mystery of Cliff Castle."

"Yes, we soon found out the secret," said Peter.

But it hadn't quite ended. The Princess of Larreeanah was so overjoyed at the recovery of her jewels that she came herself to see the three adventurous children.

She arrived in a magnificent car, and was wearing some of the jewels. Much to the children's embarrassment, she kissed them all.

They didn't like being kissed by strangers, even if this stranger was a princess, and they made up their minds they weren't going to like her. But they soon changed that idea when they found what she had brought for them in a small van that followed her car!

"Open the door of the van and see what is inside for you!" she said to the three surprised children. Brock pulled open the doors at the back of the van and all three stared in amazement and awe at the Princess's wonderful present.

"It's a car – a small car just big enough to take the three of us!" said Brock, staring at the marvellous little car inside the van. It was bright red, with yellow bands and yellow spokes to the wheels. The lights, windscreen and handles shone like silver.

"It goes by electricity," said the princess. "I had it made especially for you. You don't have to have a driving licence, of course, because it is listed as a toy car. But actually it is driven just like a real one, has a horn and everything, and as it goes by electricity, you don't need petrol."

"Let's go for a ride in it now!" shouted Peter in excitement. So they pulled out the magnificent little car and got into it. Brock drove it. He pulled a lever, took hold of the steering wheel, and off went the car down the lane with its three excited passengers.

"What a wonderful end to an adventure!" cried Peter. "Didn't I say we'd have real, proper adventures? And wasn't I right?"

Well – he certainly was!

SMUGGLER BEN

1

The Cottage by the Sea

On a summer's day in 1943, three children got out of a bus and looked around them in excitement. Their mother smiled to see their glowing faces.

"Well, here we are!" she said. "How do you like it?"

"Is this the cottage we're going to live in for four weeks?" said Alec, going up to the little white gate. "Mother! It's perfect!"

The two girls, Hilary and Frances, looked at the small square cottage, and agreed with their brother. Red roses climbed all over the cottage, even to the chimneys. The thatched roof came down low over the ground floor windows, and in the thatch itself other little windows jutted out.

"I wonder which is our bedroom," said Hilary, looking up at the roof. "I hope that one is because it will look out over the sea."

"Well, let's go in and see," said the children's mother. "Help with the suitcases, Alec. I hope the heavy luggage has already arrived."

They opened the white gate of Sea Cottage and went up the little stone path. It was set with orange marigolds at each side, and hundreds of the bright red-gold flowers looked up at the children as they passed.

The cottage was very small inside. The front door opened straight on to the little sitting-room. Beyond was a tiny dark kitchen. To the left was another room, whose walls were covered with bookshelves lined with books. The children stared at them in surprise.

"The man who owns this house is someone who is interested in history," said Mother, "so most of these books are about long-ago days, I expect. They belong to Professor Rondel. He said that you might dip into any of the books if you liked, on condition that you put them back very carefully in the right place."

"Well, I don't think I shall want to do any dipping into these books!" said Hilary.

"No – dipping in the sea will suit you better!" Frances said, laughing. "Mother, let's see our bedrooms now."

They went upstairs. There were three bedrooms, one very tiny indeed. Two were at the front and one was at the back. A small one and a large one were at the front, and a much bigger one behind.

"I shall have this big one," said Mother. "Then if your father comes down there will be plenty of room for him, too. Alec, you can have the tiny room overlooking the sea. And you two girls can have the one next to it."

"That overlooks the sea, too!" said Hilary joyfully. "But, Mother – wouldn't you like a room that looks out over the sea? Yours won't."

"I shall see the sea out of this little side window," said Mother, going to it. "And anyway, I shall get a wonderful view of the moors at the back. You know how I love them, especially now when the heather is out."

The children gazed out at the moors ablaze with purple heather. It was really a lovely spot.

"Blue sea in front and purple heather behind," said Alec. "What can anyone want better than that?"

"Well – tea for one thing," said Frances. "I'm most terribly hungry. Mother, could we have something to eat before we do anything?"

"If you like," said Mother. "We can do the unpacking afterwards. Alec, there is a tiny village down the road there, with about two shops and a few fishermen's cottages. Go with the girls and see if you can buy something for tea."

They clattered down the narrow wooden stairway and ran out of the front door and down the path between the marigolds. They went down the sandy road, where blue chicory blossomed by the wayside and red poppies danced.

"Isn't it heavenly!" cried Hilary. "We're at the seaside – and the holidays are just beginning. We've never been to such a lovely little place before. It's much, much nicer than the big places we've been to. I don't want bands and piers and things. I only want the yellow sands, and big rocky cliffs, and water as blue as this."

"I vote we go down to the beach after tea, when we've helped Mother to unpack," said Alec. "The tide will be going out then. It comes right up to the cliffs now. Look at it splashing high up the rocks!"

The children peered over the edge of the cliff and saw the white spray flying high. It was lovely to watch. The gulls soared above their heads, making laughing cries as they went.

"I would love to be a gull for a little while," said Frances longingly. "Just think how glorious it would be to glide along on the wind like that for ages and ages. Sometimes I dream I'm doing that."

"So do I," said Hilary. "It's a lovely feeling. Well, come on. It's no good standing here when we're getting things for tea. I'm awfully hungry."

"You always are," said Alec. "I never knew such a girl. All right – come on, Frances. We can do all the exploring we want to after tea."

They ran off. Sand got into their shoes, but they liked it. It was all part of the seashore and there wasn't anything by the sea that they didn't like. They felt very happy.

They came to the village – though really it could hardly be called a village. There were two shops. One was a tiny baker's, which was also the little post office. The other was a general store that sold everything from pokers to strings of sausages. It was a most fascinating shop.

"It even sells foreign stamps," said Alec, looking at some packets in the window. "And look – that's a lovely boat. I might buy that if I've got enough money."

Hilary went to the baker's. She bought a large crusty loaf, a big cake and some currant buns. She asked for the butter and jam at the other store. The little old lady who served her smiled at the children.

"So you've come to Sea Cottage, have you?" she said. "Well, I hope you have a good holiday. And mind you come along to see me every day, for I sell sweets, chocolates and ice creams, as well as all the other things you see."

"Oooh!" said Hilary. "Well, we'll certainly come and see you then!"

They had a look at the other little cottages in the

village. Fishing nets were drying outside most of them. And one or two of them were being mended. A boy of about Alec's age was mending one. He stared at the children as they passed. They didn't know whether to smile or not.

"He looks a bit fierce, doesn't he?" said Hilary. They looked back at the boy. He did look rather fierce. He was very, very dark, and his face and hands were darkly sunburned. He wore an old blue jersey and trousers, rather ragged, which he had tied up at the ankles. He was barefooted, but beside him were big sea boots.

"I don't think I like him much," said Frances. "He looks rather rough."

"Well, he won't bother us much," said Alec. "He's only a fisherboy. Anyway, if he starts to be rough, I shall be rough, too – and he won't like that!"

"You wouldn't be nearly as strong as that fisherboy," said Hilary.

"Yes, I would!" said Alec at once.

"No, you wouldn't," said Hilary. "I bet he's got muscles like iron!"

"Shut up, you two," said Frances. "It's too lovely a day to quarrel. Come on – let's get back home. I want my tea."

They sat in the garden to have their tea. Their

mother had brought out a table and stools, and the four of them sat there happily, eating big crusty slices of bread and butter and jam, watching the white tops of the blue waves as they swept up the shore.

"The beach looks a bit dangerous for bathing," said Mother. "I'm glad you are all good swimmers. Alec, you must see that you find out what times are best for bathing. Don't let the girls go in if it's dangerous."

"We can just wear bathing costumes, Mother, can't we?" said Alec. "And go barefoot?"

"Well, you won't want to go barefoot on those rocky cliffs, surely!" said Mother. "You can do as you like. But just be sensible, that's all."

"We'll help you to unpack now," said Hilary, getting up.

"Gracious, Hilary – you don't mean to say you've had enough tea yet?" said Alec, pretending to be surprised. "You've only had seven pieces of bread and jam, three pieces of cake and two currant buns!"

Hilary pulled Alec's hair hard and he yelled. Then they all went indoors. Mother said she would clear away the tea when they had gone down to the beach.

In half an hour all the unpacking was done and

the children were free to go down to the beach. The tide was now out quite a long way and there was plenty of golden sand to run on.

"Come on!" said Alec impatiently. "Let's go. We won't change into swimming things now, it will waste time. We'll go as we are!"

So off they sped, down the marigold path, through the white gate, and into the sandy lane. A small path led across the grassy cliff top to where steep steps had been cut in the cliff itself in order that people might get up and down.

"Down we go!" said Alec. "My word – doesn't the sea look grand. I've never seen it so blue in my life!"

2

A Nasty Boy

They reached the beach. It was wet from the tide and gleamed brightly as they walked on it. Their feet made little prints on it that faded almost as soon as they were made. Gleaming shells lay here and there, as pink as sunset.

There were big rocks sticking up everywhere, and around them were deep and shallow pools. The children loved paddling in them because they were so warm. They ran down to the edge of the sea and let the white edges of the waves curl over their toes. It was all lovely.

"The fishing boats are out," said Alec, shading his eyes as he saw the boats setting out on the tide, their white sails gleaming in the sun. "And listen – is that a motorboat?"

It was. One came shooting by at a great pace, and then another. They came from the big seaside town not far off where many trippers went. The children watched them fly past, the white spray flying into the air.

They wandered along by the sea, exploring all

the rock pools, picking up shells and splashing in the edge of the water. They saw nobody at all until they rounded a rocky corner of the beach and came to a small cove, well hidden between two jutting-out arms of the cliff.

They heard the sound of whistling, and stopped. Sitting beside a small boat, doing something to it, was the fisherboy they had seen before tea.

He now had on his sea boots, a red fisherman's cap with a tassel hanging down, and a bright red scarf tied round his trousers.

"That's the same boy we saw before," said Alec.

The boy heard the sound of voices on the breeze and looked up. He scowled, and his dark face looked savage. He stood up and looked threateningly towards the three children.

"Well, he looks fiercer than ever," said Hilary, at last. "What's the matter with him, I wonder? He doesn't look at all pleased to see us."

"Let's go on and take no notice of him," said Alec. "He's no right to glare at us like that. We're doing no harm!"

So the three children walked into the hidden cove, not looking at the fisherboy at all. But as soon as they had taken three or four steps, the boy shouted at them loudly.

"Hey, you there! Keep out of this cove!"

The children stopped. "Why should we?" said Alec.

"Because it belongs to me," said the boy. "You keep out of this. It's been my cove for years, and no one's come here. I won't have you trippers coming into it and spoiling it."

"We're not trippers!" cried Hilary indignantly. "We're staying at Sea Cottage for a whole month."

"Well, you're trippers for a month then instead of for a day!" said the boy sulkily. "Clear off, I tell you! This is my own place here. I don't want anyone else in it. If you come here I'll set on you and beat you off."

The boy really looked so fierce that the children felt quite frightened. Then out of his belt he took a gleaming knife. That settled things for the two girls. They weren't going to have any quarrel with a savage boy who held such a sharp knife.

But Alec was furious. "How dare you threaten us with a knife!" he shouted. "You're a coward. I haven't a knife or I'd fight you."

"Alec! Come away!" begged Frances, clutching hold of her brother. "Do come away. I think that boy's mad. He looks it, anyway."

The boy stood watching them, feeling the sharp edge of his knife with his thumb. His sullen face looked as black as thunder.

Frances and Hilary dragged Alec off round the rocky corner. He struggled with them to get free, and they tore his shirt.

"Now look what you've done!" he cried angrily. "Let me go!"

"Alec, it's seven o'clock already and Mother said we were to be back by then," said Hilary, looking at her watch. "Let's go back. We can settle with that horrid boy another day."

Alex shook himself free and set off home with the girls rather sulkily. He felt that the evening had been spoiled. It had all been so lovely – and now that nasty boy had spoiled everything.

The girls told their mother about the boy and she was astonished. "Well, he certainly does sound rather mad," she said. "For goodness sake don't start quarrelling with him. Leave him alone."

"But, Mother, if he won't let us go into the little coves, it's not fair," said Hilary.

Mother laughed. "Don't worry about that!" she said. "There will be plenty of times when he's busy elsewhere, and the places you want to go to will be empty. Sometimes the people who live in a place do resent others coming to stay in it for a while."

"Mother, could we have a boat, do you think?" asked Alec. "It would be such fun."

"I'll go and see about one for you tomorrow," said Mother. "Now it's time you all went to bed. Hilary is yawning so widely that I can almost count her teeth!"

They were all tired. They fell into bed and went to sleep at once, although Hilary badly wanted to lie awake for a time and listen to the lovely noise the sea made outside her window. But she simply couldn't keep her eyes open, and in about half a minute she was as sound asleep as the other two.

It was lovely to wake up in the morning and remember everything. Frances woke first and sat up. She saw the blue sea shining in the distance and she gave Hilary a sharp dig.

"Hilary! Wake up! We're at the seaside!"

Hilary woke with a jump. She sat up, too, and gazed out to the sea, over which white gulls were soaring. She felt so happy that she could hardly speak. Then Alec appeared at the door in his bathing suit. He had nothing else on at all, and he looked excited.

"I'm going for a dip," he said in a low voice. "Are you coming? Don't wake Mother. It's too early."

The girls almost fell out of bed in their excitement. They pulled on swimming costumes, and then crept out of the cottage with Alec.

It was about half past six. The world looked clean and new. "Just as if it has been freshly washed," said Hilary, sniffing the sharp, salt breeze. "Look at those pink clouds over there! And did you ever see such a clear blue as the sea is this morning. Ooooh – it's cold!"

It was cold. The children ran into the water a little way and then stopped and shivered. Alec plunged right under and came up, shaking the drops from his hair. "Come on, you two!" he yelled. "It's gorgeous once you're in!"

The girls were soon right under, and the three of them spent twenty minutes swimming out and back, diving under the water and catching each other's legs, then floating happily on their backs, looking up into the clear morning sky.

"Time to come out," said Alex, at last. "Come on. Race you up the cliff!"

But they had to go slowly up the cliff, for the steps really were very steep. They burst into the cottage to find their mother up and bustling round to get breakfast ready.

At half past seven they were all having breakfast. Afterwards Mother said she would tidy round the house and then do the shopping. The girls and Alex must make their own beds, just as they did at home.

"When we are down in the village I'll make inquiries about a boat for you," promised Mother, when at last the beds were made, the kitchen and sitting-room tidied and set in order. "Now are we ready? Bring that big basket, Alec, I shall want that."

"Mother, we must buy spades," said Alec. "That sand would be gorgeous to dig in."

"Gracious! Aren't you too big to dig?" said Mother. The children laughed.

"Mother, you're not too big either! Don't you remember how you helped us to dig that simply enormous castle last year, with the big moat round it? It had steps all the way up it and was simply lovely."

They set off joyously, Alec swinging the basket. They did a lot of shopping at the little general store, and the little old lady beamed at them.

"Do you know where I can arrange about hiring a boat for my children?" Mother asked her.

"Well," said the old lady, whose name was Mrs Polsett, "I really don't know. We use all our boats hereabouts, you know. You could ask Samuel. He lives in the cottage over yonder. He's got a small boat as well as a fishing boat. Maybe he'd let the children have it."

So Mother went across to where Samuel was sitting mending a great fishing net. He was an old man with bright blue eyes and a wrinkled face like a shrivelled brown apple.

"Have you a boat I could hire for my children?" Mother asked.

Samuel shook his head. "No," he said. "I have got one, it's true, but I'm not hiring it out any more. Some boys had it last year, and they lost the oars and made a great hole in the bottom. I lost more money on that there boat than I made."

"Well, I'm sure my three children would be very careful indeed," said Mother, seeing the disappointed faces around her. "Won't you lend it to them for a week and see how they get on? I will pay you well."

"No, thank you kindly," said Samuel firmly.

"Is there anyone else who has a boat to spare?" said Alec, feeling rather desperate, for he had really set his heart on a boat.

"No one that I know of," said Samuel. "Some of us lost our small boats in a big storm this year, when the sea came right over the cliffs, the waves were so big. Maybe I'll take the children out in my fishing boat if they're well behaved."

"Thank you," said Hilary. But they all looked very disappointed, because going out in somebody else's boat wasn't a bit the same as having their own.

"We'll just go back to the shop and see if she knows of anyone else with a boat," said Mother. So back they went.

But the old lady shook her head.

"The only other person who has a boat – and it's not much of a boat, all patched and mended," she said, "is Smuggler Ben."

"Smuggler Ben!" said Alex. "Is there a smuggler here? Where does he live?"

"Oh, he's not a real smuggler!" said Mrs Polsett, with a laugh. "He's my grandson. But he's just mad on tales of the old smugglers, and he likes to pretend he's one. There were smugglers' caves here, you know, somewhere about the beach. I dare say Ben knows them. Nobody else does now."

The children felt terribly excited. Smugglers – and caves! And who was Smuggler Ben? They felt that they would very much like to know him. And he had a boat, too. He would be a grand person to know!

"Is Smuggler Ben grown-up?" asked Alec.

"Bless you, no!" said Mrs Polsett. "He's much the same age as you. Look – there he goes – down the street there!"

The children turned to look. And as soon as they saw the boy, their hearts sank.

"It's the nasty boy with the knife!" said Hilary sadly. "He won't lend us his boat."

"Don't you worry about his knife," said old Mrs Polsett. "It's all pretence with him. He's just play-acting most of the time. He always wishes he could have been a smuggler, and he's forever pretending he is one. There's no harm in him. He's a good boy for work – and when he wants to play, well, let him play as he likes, I say! He doesn't get into mischief like most boys do. He goes off exploring the cliffs, and rows in his boat half the time. But he does keep himself to himself. Shall I ask him if he'll lend you his boat sometimes?"

"No, thank you," said Alec politely. He was sure the boy would refuse rudely, and Alec wasn't going to give him the chance to do that.

They walked back to Sea Cottage. They felt sad about the boat – but their spirits rose as they saw their swimming costumes lying on the grass, bone-dry.

"What about another swim before lunch?" cried Alec. "Come on, Mother. You must come, too!"

So down to the sea they all went again, and by the squeals, shrieks and shouts, four people had a really wonderful time!

3

Hilary Has an Adventure

One evening, after tea, Frances and Alec wanted to go for a long walk. "Coming, Hilary?" they said. Hilary shook her head.

"No," she said. "I'm a bit tired with all my swimming today. I'll take a book and go and sit on the cliff top till you come back."

So Alex went off with Frances, and Hilary took her book and went to find a nice place to sit. She could see miles and miles of restless blue sea from the cliff. It was really marvellous. She walked on the cliff edge towards the east, found a big gorse bush and sat down beside it for shelter. She opened her book.

When she looked up, something nearby caught her eye. It looked like a little worn path going straight to the cliff edge. "A rabbit path, I suppose," said Hilary to herself. "But fancy the rabbits going right over the steep cliff edge like that! I suppose there must be a hole there that they pop into."

She got up to look – and to her great surprise

saw what looked like a narrow, rocky path going down the cliff side, very steep indeed! In a sandy ledge a little way down was the print of a bare foot.

"Well, someone has plainly gone down this steep path!" thought Hilary. "I wonder who it was. I wonder where it leads to. I've a good mind to find out!"

She began to go down the path. It really was very steep and rather dangerous. At one extremely dangerous part someone had driven in iron bars and stretched a piece of strong rope from bar to bar. Hilary was glad to get hold of it, for her feet were sliding down by themselves and she was afraid she was going to fall.

When she was about three-quarters of the way down she heard the sound of someone whistling very quietly. She stopped and tried to peer down to see who was on the beach.

"Why, this path leads down to that little cove we saw the other day!" she thought excitedly. "The one where the rude boy was. Oh, I hope he isn't there now!"

He was! He was sitting on his upturned boat, whittling at something with his sharp knife. Hilary turned rather pale when she saw the knife. It was all very well for old Mrs Polsett to say that her grandson was only play-acting, but Hilary was sure that Ben really felt himself to be somebody fierce – and he might act like that, too.

As she stood and watched him, unseen, she saw the sharp knife slip. The boy gave a cry of pain and clutched his left hand. He had cut it very badly indeed. Blood began to drip on to the sand.

The boy felt in his pocket for something to bind up his hand. But he could find nothing. He pressed the cut together, but it went on bleeding. Hilary was tender-hearted and she couldn't bear to see the boy's face all screwed up in pain, and do nothing about it.

She forgot to be afraid of him. She went down the last piece of cliff and jumped down on the sand. The boy heard her and turned, his face one big scowl. Hilary ran up to him.

She had a big clean handkerchief in her pocket, and she took this out. "I'll tie up your hand for you," she said. "I say – what an awful cut! I should howl like anything if I did that to myself."

The boy scowled at her again. "What are you doing here?" he said. "Where are the others?"

"I'm alone," said Hilary. "I found that funny steep path and came down it to see where it led to. And I saw you cut your hand. Give it to me. Come on, Ben – hold it out and let me tie it up. You might bleed to death if you go on like this."

The boy held out his cut hand. "How do you know my name is Ben?" he said in a surly voice.

"Never mind how I know!" said Hilary. "You're Smuggler Ben! What a marvellous name! Don't you wish you really were a smuggler? I do! I'm just reading a book about smuggling and it's terribly exciting."

"What book?" asked the boy.

Hilary bound up his hand well, and then showed him the book. "It's all about hidden caves and smugglers coming in at night and things like that," she said. "I'll lend it to you if you like."

The boy stared at her. He couldn't help liking this little girl with her honest eyes and clear, kind little voice. His hand felt much more comfortable now, too. He was grateful to her. He took the book and looked through the pages.

"I'd like to read it after you," he said more graciously. "I can't get enough books. Do you really like smuggling and that kind of thing?"

"Of course," said Hilary. "I like anything adventurous like that. Is it true that there are smugglers' caves along this coast somewhere?"

The boy stopped before he answered. "If I tell you, will you keep it a secret?" he said, at last.

"Well – I could tell the others, couldn't I?" said

Hilary. "We all share everything, you know, Alec and Frances and I."

"No, I don't want you to tell anyone," said the boy. "It's my own secret. I wouldn't mind sharing it with you, because you've helped me, and you like smuggling, too. But I don't want the others to know."

"Then don't tell me," said Hilary, disappointed. "You see, it would be mean of me to keep an exciting thing like that from the others. I just couldn't do it. You'd know how I feel if you had brothers and sisters. You just have to share exciting things."

"I haven't got any brothers or sisters," said the boy. "I wish I had. I always play alone. There aren't any boys of my age in our village – only girls, and I don't like girls. They're silly."

"Oh well, if you think that, I'll go," said Hilary, offended. She turned to go, but the boy caught her arm.

"No, don't go. I didn't mean that you were silly. I don't think you are. I think you're sensible. Let me tell you one of my secrets."

"Not unless I can share it with the others," said Hilary. "I'm simply longing to know but I don't want to leave the others out of it."

"Are they as sensible as you are?" asked Ben.

"Of course," said Hilary. "As a matter of fact, Frances, my sister, is nicer than I am. I'm always losing my temper and she doesn't. You can trust us, Ben, really you can."

"Well," said Ben slowly, "I'll let you all into my secret then. I'll show you something that will make you stare! Come here tomorrow, down that little path. I'll be here, and just see if I don't astonish you."

Hilary's eyes shone. She felt excited. She caught hold of Ben's arm and looked at him eagerly.

"You're a sport!" she said. "I like you, Smuggler Ben. Let's all be smugglers, shall we?"

Ben smiled for the first time. His brown face changed completely, and his dark eyes twinkled. "All right," he said. "We'll all be. That would be more fun than playing alone, if I can trust you all not to say a word to any grown-up. They might interfere. And now I'll tell you one little secret – and you can tell the others if you like. I know where the old smugglers' caves are!"

"Ben!" cried Hilary, her eyes shining with excitement. "Do you really? I wondered if you did. Oh, I say, isn't that simply marvellous! Will you show us them tomorrow? Oh, do say you will."

"You wait and see," said Ben. He turned his boat the right way up and dragged it down the beach.

"Where are you going?" called Hilary.

"Back home in my boat," said Ben. "I've got to go out fishing with my uncle tonight. Would you like to come back in my boat with me? It'll save you climbing up that steep path."

"Oh, I'd love to!" said Hilary joyfully. "You know, Ben, we tried and tried to hire a boat of our own, but we couldn't. We were so terribly disappointed. Can I get in? You push her out."

Ben pushed the boat out on to the waves and then got in himself. But when he took the oars he found that his cut hand was far too painful to handle the left oar. He bit his lip and went a little pale under his tan.

"What's the matter?" said Hilary. "Oh, it's your hand. Well, let me take the oars. I can row. Yes, I can, Ben! You'll only make your cut bleed again."

Ben gave up his seat and the girl took the oars. She rowed very well indeed, and the oars cut cleanly into the water. The boat flew along over the waves.

"You don't row badly for a girl," said Ben.

"Well, we live near a river at home," said Hilary, "and we're often out in our uncle's boat. We can all row. So you can guess how disappointed we were when we found that we couldn't get a boat here for ourselves."

Ben was silent for a little while. Then he spoke again. "Well — I don't mind lending you my boat sometimes, if you like. When I'm out fishing, you can have it, but don't you dare to spoil it in any way. I know it's only an old boat, but I love it."

Hilary stopped rowing and looked at Ben in delight. "I say, you really are a brick!" she said. "Do you mean it?"

"I always mean what I say," said Ben gruffly. "You lend me your books and I'll lend you my boat."

Hilary rowed all round the cliffs until she came to the beach she knew. She rowed inshore and they got out. She and Ben pulled the boat right up the beach and turned it upside down.

"I must go now," said Ben. "My uncle's waiting for me. See you tomorrow."

He went off, and Hilary turned to go home. At the top of the beach she saw Frances and Alec staring at her in amazement.

"Hilary! Were you with that awful boy in his boat?" cried Frances. "However did you dare?"

"He isn't awful after all," said Hilary. "He's quite nice. He's got wonderful secrets – simply wonderful. And he says we can use his boat when he doesn't want it!"

The other two stared open-mouthed. They simply couldn't believe all this. Why, that boy had threatened them with a knife – he couldn't possibly be nice enough to lend them his boat.

"I'll tell you all about it," said Hilary, as they set off up the cliff path. "You see, I found a little secret way down to that cove we saw – and Ben was there." She told them the whole story and they listened in silence.

"Things always happen to you, Hilary," said Frances rather enviously. "Well, I must say this is all very exciting. I can hardly wait till tomorrow. Do you really think Smuggler Ben will show us those caves? I wonder where they are? I hope they aren't miles away!"

"Well, we'll see," said Hilary happily. They went home hungry to their supper – and in bed that night each of them dreamed of caves and smugglers and all kinds of exciting things. This holiday promised to be more exciting than they had imagined.

4

An Exciting Evening

The children told their mother about Ben. She was amused.

"So the fierce little boy has turned out to be quite ordinary after all!" she said. "Well, I must say I'm glad. I didn't very much like to think of a little savage rushing about the shore armed with a sharp knife. I think it's very nice of him to lend you his boat. You had better bring him in to a meal, and then I can see him for myself."

"Oh, thanks, Mother," said Hilary. "I say – do you think we could get ourselves some fishermen's hats, like Ben wears, and have you got a bright-coloured scarf or sash that you could lend us, Mother? Or three, if you've got them. We're going to play smugglers, and it would be fun to dress up a bit. Ben does. He looks awfully grand in his tasselled hat and sash and big boots."

"Hilary, you don't seriously think I am going to hand you out all my precious scarves, do you?" said Mother. "I'll give you some money to go and buy three cheap hats and scarves with, if you like

– and you can all wear your wellingtons if you want big boots. But I draw the line at getting you sharp knives like Ben. Look how even he cut himself today!"

The children were delighted to think they could buy something they could dress up in. The next morning they set off to Mrs Polsett's and asked to see fishermen's hats. She had a few and brought them out. "I knitted them myself," she said. "Here's a red one with a yellow tassel. That would suit you fine, Hilary."

So it did. Hilary pulled it on and swung the tasselled end over her left ear just as she had seen Ben do.

Frances chose a blue one with a red tassel and Alec chose a green one with a brown tassel. Then they bought some very cheap scarves to tie round their waists.

They went back home, pulled on their wellingtons, and put on their hats and sashes.

They looked grand.

Hilary showed them where the little narrow path ran down the steep cliff.

"Goodness," said Alex, peering over the edge. "What a terrifying way down! I feel half afraid of falling. I'm sure I'll never get down those steep bits."

"There's a rope tied there," said Hilary, going down first. "Come on. Ben will be waiting. I saw his boat out on the water as we came along the cliff."

They all went down the path slowly for fear of falling. When they jumped down the last rocky step into the little cove, they saw Ben there waiting for them, sitting on his little boat. He was dressed just as they were, except that his boots were real sea boots, and he wore trousers tucked well down into them. He didn't move as they came up, nor did he smile.

"Hello, Ben!" said Hilary. "I've brought my brother and sister as you said I could. This is Alec, and this is Frances. I've told them what you said. We're all terribly excited."

"Did you tell them it's all a deep secret?" said Ben, looking at Hilary. "They won't give it away?"

"Of course we won't," said Alec indignantly. "That would spoil all the fun. I say – can we call you Smuggler Ben? It sounds splendid."

Ben looked pleased. "Yes, you can," he said. "And remember, I'm the captain. You've got to obey my orders."

"Oh," said Alec, not liking this idea quite so much. "Well – all right. Lead on. Show us your secret."

"You know, don't you, that there really were smugglers here in the old days?" said Ben. "They came up the coast quietly on dark nights, bringing in all kinds of goods. Folk here knew they came, but they were afraid of them. They used to take the goods to the old caves here, and hide them there till they could get rid of them overland."

"And do you really know where the caves are?" said Alec eagerly. "My word, Smuggler Ben — you're a wonder!"

Smuggler Ben smiled and his brown face changed at once. "Come on," he said. "I'll show you something that will surprise you!"

He led the way up the beach to the cliffs at the back. "Now," he said, "the entrance to the old caves is somewhere in this little cove. Before I show you, see if you can find it!"

"In the cove!" cried Hilary. "Oh, I guess we shall soon find it then!"

The three children began to hunt carefully along the rocky cliff. They ran into narrow caves and out again. They came to a big cave, went into that and came out again. It seemed nothing but a large cave, narrowing at the back. There were no more caves after that one, and the children turned in disappointment to Ben.

"You don't mean that these little caves and that

one big one are the old smuggling caves do you?" said Hilary. "Because they are just like heaps of other caves we have seen at the seaside."

"No, I don't mean that," said Ben. "Now, you come with me and I'll show you something exciting."

He led them into the big cave. He took them to the right of it and then jumped up to a rocky ledge which was just about shoulder high. In half a moment he had completely disappeared! Hilary felt about up the ledge and called to him in bewilderment.

"Ben! Smuggler Ben! Where have you gone?"

There was no answer. The three children stared up at the ledge. Alec jumped up to it. He felt all along it, up and down and sideways. He simply couldn't imagine where Ben had gone to!

There was a low laugh behind them. The children turned in surprise – and there was Ben, standing at the entrance to the big cave, laughing all over his brown face at their surprise.

"Ben! What happened? Where did you disappear to? And how did you get back to the entrance without us seeing you?" cried Hilary. "It's like magic. Do tell us. Quick!"

"Well, I'll show you," said Ben. "I found it out quite by accident. One day I came into this cave and fell asleep. When I woke up, the tide was high and was already coming into the cave. I was trapped. I couldn't possibly get out, because I knew I'd be dashed against the rocks outside, the sea was so stormy."

"So you climbed up on to this ledge!" cried Hilary.

"Yes, I did," said Ben. "It was the only thing to do. I just hoped and hoped the sea wouldn't fill the cave up completely, or I knew I'd be drowned. Well, I crouched there for ages, the sea getting higher and higher up till it reached the ledge."

"Gracious!" said Frances, shivering. "You must have been afraid."

"I was, rather," said Ben. "Well, I rolled right to the back of the ledge, and put up my hand to catch hold of any bit of jutting-out rock that I could – and instead of knocking against rock, my hand went into space!"

"What do you mean?" said Alec in astonishment.

"Come and see," said Ben, and he took a torch out of his pocket. All the children climbed on to the ledge and squeezed together there, watching the beam of Ben's torch. He directed it upwards – and then, to their amazement, they saw a perfectly round hole going upwards right at the far corner of the rocky ledge. It didn't look very big.

"See that?" said Ben. "Well, when I felt my hand going up that hole I slid over to this corner and put my arm right up the hole. And this is what I found."

He shone his torch up the rounded hole in the rock. The three children peered up, one after another.

Driven into the rock were great thick nails, one above the other. "See those?" said Ben. "Well, I reckon they were put there by some old smuggler."

"Did you get up the hole?" asked Alec.

"You bet I did!" said Ben. "And pretty quick, too, for the sea was washing over the ledge by that time and I was soaked through. I squeezed myself up, got my feet on those nails – they're sort of steps up, you see – and climbed up the hole by feeling for the nails with my feet."

"Where does the hole lead to?" asked Frances in excitement.

"You'd better come and see," said Ben, with a sudden grin. The children asked nothing better than that, and at once Alec put his head up the hole. It was not such a tight fit as he expected. He was easily able to climb up. There were about twenty nails for footholds and then they stopped. There was another ledge to climb out on. The boy dragged himself there, and looked down.

"Can't see a thing!" he called. "Come on up, Smuggler Ben, and bring your torch."

"I'll give Hilary my torch," said Ben. "She can shine it for you up there when she's up, and shine it down for us to climb up by, too. Go on, Hilary."

So Hilary went up next with the torch – and when she shone it around her at the top, she and Alec gave a shout of astonishment.

They were on a ledge near the ceiling of a most enormous cave. It looked almost as big as a church

to the children. The floor was of rock, not of sand. Strange lights shone in the walls. They came from the twinkling bits of metal in the rocks.

"Frances! Hurry," cried Hilary. "It's marvellous here."

Soon all four children were standing on the ledge, looking down into the great cave. In it, on the floor, were many boxes of all kinds – small, big, square, oblong. Bits of rope were scattered about, too, and an old broken lantern lay in a corner.

"Real smugglers have been here!" said Hilary in a whisper.

"What are you whispering for?" said Alec with a laugh. "Afraid they will hear you?"

"No – but it all seems so mysterious," said Hilary. "Let's get down to the floor of the cave. How do we get there?"

"Climb down and then jump," said Ben.

So they climbed and jumped. They ran to the boxes and opened the lids.

"No good," said Ben. "I've done that long ago. They're quite empty. I often come to play smugglers here when I'm by myself. Isn't it a great place?"

"Simply marvellous!" said Alec. "Let's all come here and play tomorrow. We can bring candles and something to eat and drink. It would be gorgeous."

"Oooh, yes," said Hilary. So they planned everything in excitement, and then climbed back to the ledge, and down through the hole into the first cave. Out they went into the sunshine. Ben smiled as much as the rest.

"It's fun to share my secret with you," he told the others half shyly. "It will be grand to play smugglers all together, instead of just by myself. I'll bring some sandwiches tomorrow, and some plums. You bring anything you can, too. It shall be our own secret smugglers' cave – and we're the smugglers!"

5

Yet Another Secret

The next day the four children met together in the big cave. They felt very excited as they climbed up the hole and then jumped down into the smugglers' cave. They had brought candles and food with them, and Alec had bottles of home-made lemonade on his back in a leather bag.

They played smugglers to their hearts' content. Ben ordered them about, and called them "My men", and everyone enjoyed the game thoroughly. At last, Alec sat down on a big box and said he was tired of playing.

"I'd like something to eat," he said. "Let's use this big box for a table."

They set the things out on the table. And then Hilary looked in a puzzled way at the box.

"What's up?" asked Alec, seeing her look.

"Well, I'm just wondering something," said Hilary. "How in the world did the smugglers get this big box up the small round hole to this cave? After all, that hole only just takes us comfortably – surely this box would never have got through it."

Frances and Alec stared at the box. They felt puzzled, too. It was quite certain that no one could have carried such a big box through the hole. They looked at Ben.

"Have you ever thought of that?" Alec asked him.

"Plenty of times," said Ben. "And, what's more, I know the answer!"

"Tell us!" begged Hilary. "Is there another way into this cave?"

Smuggler Ben nodded. "Yes," he said. "I'll show it to you if you like. I just wanted to see if any of my three men were clever enough to think of such a thing. Come on – I'll show you the other way in. Didn't you wonder yesterday how it was that I came back into the other cave after I'd disappeared up the hole?"

He stood up and the others rose, too, all excited. Ben went to the back of the cave. It seemed to the children as if the wall there was quite continuous – but it wasn't. There was a fold in it – and in the fold was a passage! It was wide, but low, and the children had to crouch down almost double to get into it. But almost immediately it rose high and they could stand. Smuggler Ben switched on his torch, and the children saw that the passage was quite short and led into yet another cave. This was small and ran right down to the rocky side of the cliff very steeply, more like a wide passage than a cave.

The children went down the long cave and came to a rocky inlet of water. "When the tide comes in, it sweeps right through this cave," said Ben, "and I reckon that this is where the smugglers brought in their goods – by boat. The boat would be guided into this watery passage at high tide, and beached at the far end, where the tide didn't reach. Then the things could easily be taken into the big cave. The smugglers left a way of escape for themselves down the hole we climbed through from the first cave – you know, where the nails are driven into the rock."

"This gets more and more exciting!" said Alec. "Anything more, Ben? Don't keep it from us. Tell us everything!"

"Well, there is one thing more," said Ben, "but it just beats me. Maybe the four of us together could do something about it, though. Come along and I'll show you."

He led them back to the little passage between the big cave and the one they were in. He climbed up the wall a little way and then disappeared. The others followed him.

There was another passage leading off into the

darkness there, back into the cliff. Ben shone his torch down it as the others crowded on his heels.

"Let's got up it!" cried Alec excitedly.

"We can't," said Ben, and he shone his torch before him. "The passage walls have fallen in just along there – look!"

So they had. The passage ended in a heap of stones, soil and sand. It was completely blocked up.

"Can't we clear it?" cried Alec.

"Well, we might, as there are so many of us," said Ben. "I didn't feel like tackling it all by myself, I must say. For one thing I didn't know how far back the passage was blocked. It might have fallen in for a long way."

"I wonder where it leads to," said Alec. "It seems to go straight back. I say – isn't this exciting!"

"We'll come and dig it out tomorrow," said Hilary, her eyes dancing. "We'll bring our spades – and a sack or something to put the stones and soil in. Then we can drag it away and empty it."

"Be here tomorrow after tea," said Smuggler Ben, laughing. "I'll bring my uncle's big spade. That's a powerful one – it will soon dig away the soil."

So the next day the children crowded into the cave with spades and sacks. They used the ordinary way in, climbing up the hole by the nails and getting into the cave from the high ledge. Then they made their way into the low passage, and climbed up where the roof rose high, till they came to the blocked-up passage. They went on by the light of their torches and came to the big fall of stones and soil.

"Now, men, to work!" said Smuggler Ben, and the gang set to work with a will. The boys shovelled away the soil and stones, and the girls filled the sacks. Then the boys dragged them down the passage, let them fall into the opening between the two caves, climbed down, dragged the sacks into the large cave and emptied them into a corner. Then back they went again to do some more digging.

"What's the time?" said Alec, at last. "I feel as if we've been working for hours. We mustn't forget that high tide is at half past seven. We've got to get out before then."

Hilary looked at her watch. "It's all right," she said. "It's only half past six. We've plenty of time."

"Gracious! Hasn't the time gone slowly!" said Frances in surprise. "Come on – we can do a lot more!"

They went on working, and after a time Ben began to feel rather uncomfortable. "Hilary, what's the time now?" he said. "I'm sure it must be getting near high tide."

Hilary glanced at her watch again. "It's half past six," she said in surprise.

"But you said that before!" cried Ben. "Has your watch stopped?"

It had! Hilary held it to her ear and cried out in dismay. "Yes! It's stopped. Oh no! I wonder what the right time is."

"Quick! We'd better go and see how the tide is," said Ben, and he dropped his spade and rushed to the entrance of the blocked-up passage. He dropped down and went into the big cave, and then climbed up to the ledge, and then down by the nail studded hole on to the ledge in the first cave.

But even as he climbed down to the ledge, he felt the wash of water over his foot. "Gosh! The tide's almost in!" he yelled. "We're caught! We can't get out!"

He climbed back and stood in the big cave with the others. They looked at him, half frightened.

"Don't be scared," said Smuggler Ben. "It only means we'll have to wait a few hours till the tide goes down. I hope your mother won't worry."

"She's out tonight," said Alec. "She won't know. Does the water come in here, Ben?"

"Of course not," said Ben. "This cave is too high up. Well – let's sit down, have some chocolate and a rest, and then, we might as well get on with our job."

Time went on. The boys went to see if the tide was falling, but it was still very high. It was getting dark outside. The boys stood at the end of the long, narrow cave, up which the sea now rushed deeply. And as they stood there, they heard a strange noise coming nearer and nearer.

"Whatever's that?" said Alec in astonishment.

"It sounds like a motorboat," said Ben.

"It can't be," said Alec.

But it was. A small motorboat suddenly loomed out of the darkness and worked itself very carefully up the narrow passage and into the long cave, which was now full of deep water! The boys were at first too startled to move. They heard men and women talking in low voices.

"Is this the place?"

"Yes – step out just there. Wait till the wave goes back. That's it – now step out."

Ben clutched hold of Alec's arm and pulled him silently away, back into the entrance between the caves. Up they went in the blocked passage. The girls called out to them: "What's the tide like?"

"Sh!" said Smuggler Ben, so fiercely that the

girls were quite frightened. They stared at Ben with big eyes. The boy told them in a whisper what he and Alec had seen.

"Something's going on," he said mysteriously. "I don't know what. But it makes me suspicious when strange motorboats come to our coasts late at night like this and run into a little-known cave. After all, our country is at war – they may be up to no good, these people. They may be enemies!"

All the children felt a shivery feeling down their backs when Ben said this. Hilary felt that it was just a bit too exciting. "What do you mean?" she whispered.

"I don't exactly know," said Ben. "All I know for certain is that it's plain somebody else knows of these caves and plans to use them for something. I don't know what. And it's up to us to find out!"

"Oooh! I wish we could!" said Hilary, at once. "What are we going to do now? Wait here?"

"Alec and I will go down to the beginning of this passage," said Ben. "Maybe the people don't know about it. We'll see if we can hear what they say."

So they crept down to the beginning of the passage and leaned over to listen. Three or four people had now gone into the big cave, but to Ben's great disappointment they were talking a strange language, and he could not understand a word. Then came something he did understand! One of the women spoke in English. "We will bring them on Thursday night," she said. "When the tide is full."

Another man answered. Then the people went back to their motorboat, and the boys soon heard the whirring of the engine as it made its way carefully out of the long, narrow cave.

"They're using that cave rather like a boathouse," said Ben. "Golly, I wonder how they knew about it. And what are they bringing in on Thursday night?"

"Smuggled goods, do you think?" said Alec, hot with excitement. "People always smuggle things in wartime. Mother said so. They're smugglers, Ben – smugglers of nowadays! And they're using the old smugglers' cave again. I say – isn't this awfully exciting?"

"Yes, it is," said Smuggler Ben. "We'd better come here on Thursday night, Alec. We'll have to see what happens. We simply must. Can you slip away at about midnight, do you think?"

"Of course!" said Alec. "You bet! And the girls, too! We'll all be here! And we'll watch to see exactly what happens. Fancy spying on real smugglers, Ben. How exciting!"

6

A Strange Discovery

Mother was in by the time the children got back home, and she was very worried indeed about them.

"Mother, it's all right," said Alec, going over to her. "We just got caught by the tide, that's all, playing in caves. But we were quite safe. We just waited till the tide went down."

"Now listen, Alec," said Mother, "this just won't do. I shall forbid you to play in those caves if you get caught another time and worry me like this. I imagined you all drowning or something."

"We're awfully sorry, Mother," said Hilary, putting her arms round her. "Really, we wouldn't have worried you for anything. Look – my watch stopped at half past six, and that put us all wrong about the tide."

"Very well," said Mother. "I'll forgive you this time – but I warn you, if you worry me again like this you won't be allowed to set foot in a single cave!"

The next day it poured with rain, which was

very disappointing. Alec ran down to the village to see what Ben was doing. The two girls talked excitedly about what had happened the night before.

"Mother says will you come and spend the day with us?" said Alec. "Do come. You'll like Mother, she's a dear."

The two boys went back to Sea Cottage. The girls welcomed them, and Mother shook hands with Ben very politely. "I'm glad you can come for the day," she said. "You'd better go up to the girls' bedroom and play there. I want the sitting-room to do some writing in this morning."

So they all went up to the bedroom above, and sat down to talk. "It's nice of Mother to send us up here," said Hilary. "We can talk in peace. What are our plans for Thursday, Captain?"

"Well, I don't quite know," said Ben slowly. "You see, we've got to be there at midnight, haven't we? – but we simply must be there a good time before that, because of the tide. You see, we can't get into either cave if the tide is up. We'd be dashed to pieces."

The children stared at Smuggler Ben in dismay. None of them had thought of that.

"What time would we have to be there?" asked Alec.

"We'd have to be there about half past nine, as far as I can reckon," said Ben. "Can you leave by that time? What would your mother say?"

"Mother wouldn't let us, I'm sure of that," said Hilary in disappointment. "She was so dreadfully worried about us last night. I'm quite sure if we told her what we wanted to do, she would say no at once."

"She isn't in bed by that time, then?" said Ben.

The children shook their heads. All four were puzzled and disappointed. They couldn't think how to get over the difficulty. There was no way out of the cottage except through the sitting-room door – and Mother would be in the room, writing or reading, at the time they wanted to go out.

"What about getting out of the window?" said Alec, going over to look. But that was quite impossible, too. It was too far to jump, and, anyway, Mother would be sure to hear any noise they made.

"It looks as if I'll have to go alone," said Ben gloomily. "It's funny – I used to like doing everything all by myself, you know, but I don't like it now at all. I want to be with my three men!"

"Oh, Ben, it would be awful thinking of you down in those caves finding out what was happening – and us in our beds, wanting and longing to be with you!" cried Hilary.

"Well, I simply don't know what else to do," said Ben. "If you can't come, you can't. And certainly I wouldn't let you come after your mother had gone to bed, because by that time the tide would be up, and you'd simply be washed away as soon as you set foot on the beach. No – I'll go alone, and I'll come and tell you what's happened the next morning."

The children felt terribly disappointed and gloomy. "Let's go downstairs into the little study place that's lined with books," said Hilary, at last. "I looked into one of the books the other day, and it seemed to be all about this district in the old days. Maybe we might find some bits about smugglers."

Ben brightened up at once. "That would be fine," he said. "I know Professor Rondel was supposed to have a heap of books about this district. He was a funny man – never talked to anyone. I didn't like him."

The children went downstairs. Mother called out to them: "Where are you going?"

"Into the book room," said Hilary, opening the sitting-room door. "We can, can't we?"

"Yes, but be sure to take care of any book you use, and put it back into its right place," said Mother.

They promised this and then went into the little study.

"My word! What hundreds of books!" said Ben in amazement. The walls were lined with them, almost from floor to ceiling. The boy ran his eyes along the shelves. He picked out a book and looked at it. "Here's a book about the moors behind here," he said. "And maps, too. Look – I've been along here – and crossed that stream just there."

The children looked. "We ought to go for some walks with you over those lovely moors, Ben," said Alec. "I'd like that."

Hilary took down one or two books and looked through them, too, trying to find something exciting to read. She found nothing and put them back. Frances showed her a book on the top shelf.

"Look," she said, "do you think that would be any good? It's called *Smugglers' Haunts*."

"It might be interesting," said Hilary, and stood on a chair to get the book. It was big and old and smelled musty. The girl jumped down with it and opened it on the table. The first picture she saw made her cry out.

"Oh, look – here's an old picture of this village! Here are the cliffs – and there are the old, old houses that the fishermen still live in!"

She was quite right. Underneath the picture was

written: *A little-known smugglers' haunt. See page 66.*

They turned to page sixty-six, and found printed there an account of the caves in the little cove on the beach. *The best-known smuggler of those days was a dark, fiery man named Smuggler Ben,* said the book. The children exclaimed in surprise and looked at Ben.

"How funny!" they cried. "Did you know that, Ben?"

"No," said Ben. "My name is really Benjamin, of course, but everyone calls me Ben. I'm dark too. I wonder if Smuggler Ben was an ancestor of mine – you know, some sort of relation a hundred or more years ago."

"Quite likely," said Alec. "I wish we could find a picture of him to see if he's like you."

But they couldn't. They turned over the pages of the book and gave it up. But before they shut it Ben took hold of it. He had an idea.

"I wonder if by chance there's a mention of that blocked-up passage," he said. "It would be fun to know where it comes out, wouldn't it?"

He looked carefully through the book. He came again to page sixty-six, and looked at it closely. "Someone has written a note in the margin of this page," he said, holding it up to the light. "It's written in pencil, very faintly. I can hardly make it out."

The children did make it out at last. For more information, see page 87 of "Days of Smugglers", the note said. The children looked at one another.

"That would be a book," said Alec, moving to the shelves. "Let's see who can find it first."

Hilary found it. She was always the sharpest of the three. It was a small book, bound in black, and the print was rather faded. She turned to page eighty-seven. The book was all about the district they were staying in, and on page eighty-seven was a description of the old caves. And then came something that excited the children very much.

"Read it out, Ben, read it out!" cried Alec. "It's important."

So Ben read it out. "'From a well-hidden opening between two old smugglers' caves is a curious passage, partly natural, partly man-made, probably by the smugglers themselves. This runs steadily upwards through the cliffs, and eventually stops not far from a little stream. A well-hidden hole leads upwards on to the moor. This was probably the way the smugglers used when they took their goods from the caves, over the country.'"

The children stared at one another, trembling with excitement. "So that's where the passage goes to!" said Alec. "My word – if only we could find the other end! Ben, have you any idea at all where it ends?"

"None at all," said Ben. "But it wouldn't be very difficult to find out! We know whereabouts the beginnings of the passage are – and if we follow a more or less straight line inland till we come to a stream on the moors, we might be able to spot the hole!"

"I say! Let's go now, at once, this very minute!" cried Hilary, shouting in her excitement.

"Shut up, silly," said Alec. "Do you want to tell everyone our secrets? It's almost lunch-time. We can't go now. But I vote we go immediately afterwards!"

"Professor Rondel must have known all about

those caves," said Ben thoughtfully. "I suppose he couldn't have anything to do with the strange people we overheard last night? No — that's too far-fetched. But the whole thing is very strange. I do hope we shall be able to find the entrance to the other end of that secret passage."

Mother called the children at that moment. "Lunch!" she cried. "Come along, bookworms, and have a little something to eat."

They were all hungry. They went to wash and make themselves tidy, and then sat down and ate a most enormous meal. Ben liked the children's mother very much. She talked and laughed, and he didn't feel a bit shy of her.

"You know, Alec and the girls really thought you were going after them with that knife of yours," she said.

Ben went red. "I did feel rather fierce that day," he said, "but it's awful when people come and spoil your secret places, isn't it? Now I'm glad they came, because they're the first friends I've ever had. We're having a fine time."

Mother looked out of the window as the children finished up the last of the jam tarts.

"It's clearing up," she said. "I think you all ought to go out. It will be very wet underfoot but you can put on your wellingtons. Why don't you go out on the moors for a change?"

"Oh yes, we will!" cried all four children at once. Mother was rather astonished.

"Well, you don't usually welcome any suggestions of walking in the wet," she said. "I believe you've got some sort of secret plan!"

But nobody told her what it was!

7

Good Hunting

After lunch the children put on their boots and macs. They pulled on their sou'westers, and said goodbye to their mother, and set off.

"Now for a good old hunt," said Ben. "First let's go to the cliff that juts over my little cove. Then we'll try to make out where the passage begins underground and set off from that spot."

It wasn't long before they were over the cove. The wind whipped their faces, and overhead the clouds scudded by. Ben went to about the middle of the cliff over the cove and stood there.

"I should say that the blocked-up passage runs roughly under here," he said. "Now let's think. Does it run quite straight from where it begins? It curves a bit, doesn't it?"

"Yes, but it soon curved back again to the blocked-up part," said Alec eagerly. "So you can count it about straight to there. Let's walk in a straight line from here till we think we've come over the blocked-up bit."

They walked inland over the cliff deep in purple

heather. Then Ben stopped. "I reckon we must just about be over the blocked-up bit," he said. "Now listen – we've got to look for a stream. There are four of us. We'll all part company and go off in different directions to look for the stream. Give a yell if you find one."

Soon Alec gave a yell. "There's a kind of stream here! It runs along for a little way and then disappears into a sort of little gully. I expect it makes its way down through the cliff somewhere and springs out into the sea. Would this be the stream, do you think?"

Everyone ran to where Alec stood. Ben looked down at the little brown rivulet. It was certainly very small.

"It's been bigger once upon a time," he said, pointing to where the bed was dry and wide. "Maybe this is the one. There doesn't seem to be another, anyway."

"We'll hunt about around here for an opening of some sort," said Alec, his face red with excitement.

They all hunted about, and it was Hilary who found it – quite by accident!

She was walking over the heather, her eyes glancing round for any hole, when her foot went right through into space! She had trodden on what she thought was good solid ground, over which heather grew – but almost at once she sank on one knee as her foot went through some sort of hole!

"I say! My foot's gone through a hole here," she yelled. "Is it the one? It went right through it. I nearly sprained my ankle."

The others came up. Ben pulled Hilary up and then parted the heather to see. Certainly a big hole was there – and certainly it seemed to go down a good way.

The children tugged away at armfuls of heather and soon got the tough roots out. The sides of the hole fell away as they took out the heather. Ben switched his torch on when it was fairly large. There seemed to be quite a big drop down.

"We'd better slide down a rope," he said.

"We haven't got one," said Alec,

"I've got one round my waist," said Ben, and undid a piece of strong rope from under his red belt. A stout gorse bush stood not far off, and Ben wound it round the strong stem at the bottom, pricking himself badly but not seeming to feel it at all. "I'll go down," he said. He took hold of the rope and lay down on the heather. Then he put his legs into the hole and let himself go, holding tightly to the rope. He slid into the hole and went a good way down.

"See anything?" yelled Alec.

"Yes. There is an underground channel here of some sort!" came Ben's voice, rather muffled. "I believe we're on to the right one. Wait a minute. I'm going to kick away a bit with my feet, and get some of the loose soil away."

After a bit Ben's voice came again, full of excitement.

"Come on down! There's a kind of underground channel, worn away by water. I reckon a stream must have run here at some time."

One by one the excited children slipped down the rope. They found what Ben had said – a kind of underground channel or tunnel plainly made by water of some kind in far-off days. Ben had his torch and the others had theirs. They switched them on.

Ben led the way. It was a curious path to take. Sometimes the roof was so low that the children had to crouch down, and once they had to go on hands and knees. Ben showed them the marks of tools in places where rocks jutted into the channel.

"Those marks were made by the smugglers, I reckon," he said. "They found this way and made it into a usable passage. They must have found it difficult getting some of their goods along here."

"I expect they unpacked those boxes we saw and

carried the goods on their backs in bags or sacks," said Frances, seeing the picture clearly in her mind. "Ooooh – isn't it strange to think that heaps of smugglers have gone up this dark passage carrying smuggled goods years and years ago!"

They went on for a good way and then suddenly came to an impassable bit where the roof had fallen in. They stopped.

"Well, here we are," said Ben, "we've come to the blocked-up part once more. Now the thing is, how far along is it blocked-up – just a few yards, easy to clear – or a quarter of a mile?"

"I don't see how we can tell," said Alec. The four children stood and looked at the fallen stones and soil. It was most annoying to think they could get no further.

"I know!" said Hilary suddenly. "I know! One of us could go in at the other end of the passage and yell. Then, if we can hear anything, we shall know the blockage isn't stretching very far!"

"Good idea, Hilary," said Ben, pleased. "Yes, that really is a good idea. I'd better be the one to go because I can go quickly. It'll take me a little time, so you must be patient. I shall yell loudly when I get up to the blocked bit, and then I shall knock on some stones with my spade. We did leave the spades there, didn't we?"

"We did," said Alec. "I say – this is getting awfully exciting, isn't it?"

Ben squeezed past the others and made his way up the channel. He climbed up the rope and sped off over the heather to the cliff side. Down the narrow path he went, and jumped down into the cove.

Meanwhile, the others had sat down in the tunnel, to wait patiently for any noise they might hear.

"It will be terribly disappointing if we don't hear anything," said Frances. They waited and waited. It seemed ages to them.

And then suddenly they heard something! It was Ben's voice, rather muffled and faint, but still quite unmistakable: "Helloooo! Hellooooo!"

Then came the sharp noise of a spade on rock: Crack! Crack! Crack!

"Helloooo!" yelled back all three children, wildly excited. "Helloooo!"

"Come – and – join – me!" yelled Ben's voice. "Come – and – join – me!"

"Coming, coming, coming!" shouted Alec, Hilary and Frances, and all three scrambled back up to the entrance of the hole, swarming up the rope like monkeys.

They tore over the heather back to the cliff side

and almost fell down the steep path. Down into the cove on the sand . . . in the big cave . . . up on to the ledge . . . up the nail-studded hole . . . out on the ledge in the enormous cave . . . down to the rocky floor . . . over to the passage between the two caves . . . up the wall . . . and into the blocked-up passage where Ben was impatiently waiting for them.

"You *have* been quick," he cried. "I say, I could hear your voices quite well. The blocked piece can't stretch very far. Isn't that good? Do you feel able to tackle it hard now? If so, I believe we might clear it."

"I could tackle anything!" said Alec, taking off his mac. "I could tackle the cliff itself!"

Everyone laughed. They were all pleased and excited, and felt able to do anything, no matter how hard it was.

"What's the time?" Alec said suddenly, when they had worked hard for a time, loosening the soil and filling the sacks. "Mother's expecting us in to tea, you know."

"It's quarter past four already," said Hilary in dismay. "We must stop. But we'll come back after tea."

They sped off to their tea, and Mother had to cut another big plateful of bread and butter because they finished up every bit. Then off they went again, back to their exciting task.

"I say, I say, I say!" suddenly cried Alec, making everyone jump. "I've just thought of something marvellous."

"What?" asked everyone curiously.

"Well – if we can get this passage clear, we can come down it on Thursday night, from outside," said Alec. "We don't need to bother about the tides or anything. We can slip out at half past eleven, go to the entrance on the moor and come down here and see what's happening!"

"Gosh! I never thought of that!" cried Hilary.

Ben grinned. "That's fine," he said. "Yes – you can easily do that. You needn't disturb your mother at all. I think I'd better be here earlier, though, in case those people change their plans and come before they say. Though I don't think they will, because if they come in by motorboat they'll need high tide to get their boat into the long cave."

The children went on working at the passage. Suddenly Ben gave a shout of joy.

"We're through! My spade went right through into nothing just then! Where's my torch?"

He shone it in front of him, and the children saw that he had spoken the truth. The light of the torch shone beyond into the other side of the passage! There was only a small heap of fallen earth to manage now.

"I think we'll finish this," said Alec, though he knew the girls were tired out. "I can't leave that little bit till tomorrow! You girls can sit down and have a rest. Ben and I can tackle this last bit. It will be easy."

It was. Before another half-hour had gone by, the passage was quite clear, and the children were able to walk up and down it from end to end. They felt pleased with themselves.

"Now we'll have to wait till Thursday," sighed Alec. "Gosh, what a long time it is – a whole day and a night and then another whole day. I simply can't wait!"

But they had to. They met Ben the next day and planned everything. They could hardly go to sleep on Wednesday night, and when Thursday dawned they were all awake as early as the sun.

8

Thursday Evening

The day seemed very long indeed to the children –
but they had a lovely surprise in the afternoon.
Their father arrived, and with him he brought
their Uncle Ned. Mother rushed to the gate to
meet them as soon as she saw them, and the
children shouted for joy.

Uncle Ned said he could stay a day or two, and
Father said he would stay for a whole week.

"Where's Uncle Ned going to sleep?" asked
Alec. "In my room?"

In the ordinary way the boy would have been
very pleased at the idea of his uncle sleeping in the
same room with him – but tonight a grown-up
might perhaps spoil things.

"Ned will have to sleep on the sofa in the
sitting-room," said Mother. "I don't expect he will
mind. He's had worse places to sleep in this war!"

Both Father and Uncle Ned were in the Army. It
was lucky they had leave just when the children
were on holiday. They could share a bit of it, too!
All the children were delighted.

"I say – how are we going to slip out at half past eleven tonight if Uncle Ned is sleeping in the sitting-room?" said Hilary, when they were alone. "We shall have to be jolly careful not to wake him!"

"Well, there's nothing for it but to creep through to the door," said Alec. "And if he does wake, we'll have to beg him not to tell tales of us."

The night came at last. The children went to bed as usual, but not one of them could go to sleep. They lay waiting for the time to pass, and it passed so slowly that once or twice Hilary thought her watch must have stopped, but it hadn't.

At last half past eleven came – the time when they had arranged to leave, to go to meet Ben in the passage above the caves. Very quietly the children dressed. They all wore shorts, jerseys, their smugglers' hats, sashes and rubber boots. They stole down the stairs very softly. Not a stair creaked, not a child coughed.

The door of the sitting-room was a little open. Alec pushed it a little further and put his head in. The room was dark. On the sofa Uncle Ned was lying, his regular breathing telling the children that he was asleep.

"He's asleep," whispered Alec, in a low voice. "I'll go across first and open the door. Then you two step across quietly to me. I'll shut the door after us."

The boy went across the room to the door. He opened it softly. He had already oiled it that day, by Ben's orders, and it made no sound. A streak of moonlight came in.

Silently the three children passed out and Alec shut the door. Just as they were going through the door, their uncle woke. He opened his eyes and to his amazement saw the figures of the three children going quietly out of the open door. Then it shut.

Uncle Ned sat up with a jerk. Could he be dreaming? He opened the door and looked out. No – he wasn't dreaming. There were the three figures hurrying along to the moor in the moonlight. Uncle Ned was more astonished than he had ever been in his life before.

"Now what in the world do these kids think they are doing?" he wondered. "Little monkeys slipping out like this just before midnight. What are they up to? I'll go after them and see. Maybe they'll let me join in their prank, whatever it is. Anyway, Alec oughtn't to take his two sisters out at this time of night!"

Uncle Ned pulled on a mackintosh over his pyjamas and set out down the lane after the children. They had no idea he was some way behind them. They were thrilled because they thought they had got out so easily without being heard!

They got to the hole in the heather and by the light of their torches slid down the rope. Uncle Ned was more and more amazed as he saw one child after another slide down and disappear completely. He didn't know any hole was there, of course. He found it after a time and decided to go down it himself.

Meanwhile, the children were halfway down the passage. There they met Ben, and whispered in excitement to him. "We got out without being seen – though our uncle was sleeping on the sofa near the door! Ben, have you seen or heard anything yet?"

"Not a thing," said Ben. "But they should be here soon, because it's almost midnight and the tide is full."

They all went down to the end of the passage, and jumped down to stand at the end of the long, narrow cave. This was now full of water, and the waves rushed up it continually.

"Easy enough to float any motorboat right in," said Ben. "I wonder what they're bringing."

"Listen!" said Hilary suddenly. "I'm sure I can

hear something. Is that it?"

"It's the chug-chug of that motor-boat again," whispered Alec, a shiver going down his back. He wasn't frightened, but it was all so exciting he couldn't help trembling. The girls were the same. Their knees shook a little. Only Ben was quite still and fearless.

"Now don't switch your torches on by mistake, for goodness sake," whispered Ben, as the chugging noise came nearer. "We'll stay here till we see the boat coming into the long channel of this cave, then we'll hop up into the passage and listen hard."

The motorboat came nearer and nearer. Then as it nosed gently into the long cave with its deep inlet of water, the engine was shut off.

"Now we must go," said Ben, and the four children turned. They climbed up into the passage above the caves and stood there, listening.

People got out of the motorboat, which was apparently tied up to some rock. Torches were switched on. Ben, who was leaning over the hole from the passage, counted three people going into the big cave – two men and a woman. One of the men seemed somehow familiar to him, but he was gone too quickly for Ben to take a second look.

"Well, here we are," said a voice from the

enormous cave below. "I will leave you food and drink, and you will wait here till it is safe to go inland. You have maps to show you how to go. You know what to do. Do it well. Come back here and the motorboat will fetch you a week from now."

The children listening above could not make out at all what was happening. Who were the people? And what were the two of them to do? Alec pressed hard by Ben to listen better. His foot touched a pebble and set it rolling down into the space between the caves. Before he could stop himself he gave a low cry of annoyance.

There was instant silence in the cave. Then the first voice spoke again very sharply: "What was that? Did you hear anything?"

A wave roared up the narrow cave nearby and made a great noise. While the splashing was going on Ben whispered to Alec: "Move back up the passage, quick! You idiot, they heard you! They'll be looking for us in a minute!"

The children hurried back along the passage as quietly as they could, their hearts beating painfully. And halfway along it they bumped into somebody!

Hilary screamed. Frances almost fainted with fright. Then the somebody took their arms and said: "Now what in the world are you kids doing here at this time of night?"

"Uncle Ned, oh, Uncle Ned!" said Hilary in a faint voice. "Oh, it's marvellous to have a grownup just at this very minute to help us! Uncle Ned, something very strange is going on. Tell him, Alec."

Alec told his astonished uncle very quickly all that had happened. He listened without a word and then spoke in a sharp, stern voice that the children had never heard before.

"They're spies! They've come over from the coast of Ireland. It's just opposite here, you know. Goodness knows what they're going to do – some dirty work, I expect. We've got to stop them. Now let me think. How can we get them? Can they get away from the caves except by motorboat?"

"Only up this passage, until the tide goes down," said Ben. "Sir – listen to me. I could slip down the hole and cast off the motorboat by myself. I know how to start it up. I believe I could do it. Then you could hold this passage, couldn't you, and send Alec and the girls back to get their father. You'd have to get somebody to keep guard outside the cave as soon as the tide goes down, in case they try to escape round the cliffs."

"Leave that to me," said Uncle Ned grimly. "Can you really get away in that motorboat? If you can, you'll take their only means of escape. Well, go and try. Good luck to you. You're a brave lad!"

Ben winked at the others, who were staring at him open-mouthed. Then he slipped along down the passage again until he came to the opening. He stood there listening before he let himself down into the space between the caves. It was plain that the people there had come to the conclusion that the noise they had heard was nothing to worry about, for they were talking together. There was the clink of glasses as the boy dropped down quietly to the floor below the passage.

"They're wishing each other good luck!" said the boy to himself, with a grin. He went to the motorboat, which was gently bobbing up and down as waves ran under it up the inlet of water in the cave. He climbed quietly in. He felt about for the rope that was tied round a rock, and slipped it loose. The next wave took the boat down with it, and as soon as he dared, Ben started up the engine to take her out of the deep channel in the cave.

He was lucky in getting the boat out fairly quickly. As soon as the engine started up, there came a shout from the cave, and Ben knew that the two men there had run to see what was happening. He ducked in case there was any shooting. He guessed that the men would be desperate when they saw their boat going.

He got the boat clear, and swung her out on the water that filled the cove. The boy knew the coast almost blindfolded, and soon the little motorboat was chug-chug-chugging across the open sea towards the beach where a little jetty ran out, and where Ben could tie her up. He was filled with glee. It was marvellous to think he had beaten those men – and that woman, too, whoever she was. Spies! Well – now they knew what British boys and girls could do!

He wondered what the others were doing. He felt certain that Alec and the girls were even now speeding up the passage, climbing out through the heather and racing back home to wake their father.

And that is exactly what they were doing! They had left their uncle in the passage – and in his hand was his loaded revolver. No one could escape by that passage, even if they knew of it.

"Tell your father what you have told me, and tell him Ben has taken the boat away," Uncle Ned had instructed them. "I want men to guard the outer entrance of the caves as soon as the tide goes down. I'll remain here to guard this way of escape. Go quickly!"

9

Things Move Quickly

Alec and the two girls left their uncle and stumbled up the dark passage, lighting their way by their small torches. All three were trembling with excitement. It seemed suddenly a very serious thing that was happening. Spies! Who would have thought of that?

They went on up the passage. Soon they came to the place where the roof fell very low indeed, and down they went on their hands and knees to crawl through the low tunnel.

"I don't like that bit much," said Frances, when they were through it. "I shall dream about that! Come on – we can stand upright again now. Whatever do you suppose Daddy and Mother will say?"

"I can't imagine," said Alec. "All I know is that it's a very lucky thing for us that Dad and Uncle happened to be here now. Gosh – didn't I jump when we bumped into Uncle Ned in this passage!"

"I screamed," said Hilary, rather ashamed of herself. "But honestly I simply couldn't help it. It was awful to bump into somebody strange like that in the darkness. But wasn't I glad when I heard Uncle Ned's voice!"

"Here we are at last," said Alec, as they came to where the rope hung down the hole. "I'll go up first and then give you two girls a hand. Give me a heave, Hilary."

Hilary heaved him up and he climbed the rope quickly, hand over hand, glad that he had been so good at gym at school. You never knew when things would come in useful!

He lay down on the heather and helped the girls up. They stood out on the moor in the moonlight, getting back their breath, for it wasn't easy to haul themselves up the rope.

"Now come on," said Hilary. "We haven't any time to lose. I shouldn't be surprised if those spies know about the passage and make up their minds to try it. We don't want to leave Uncle Ned too long. After all, it's three against one."

They tore over the heather, and came to the sandy lane where Sea Cottage shone in the moonlight. They went in at the open door and made their way to their parents' bedroom. Alec hammered on the door and then went in.

His father and mother were sitting up in astonishment. They switched on the light and stared at the three children, all fully dressed as they were.

"What's the meaning of this?" asked their father. But before he could say another word the three children began to pour out their story. At first their parents could not make out what they were talking about, and their mother made the girls stop talking so that Alec could tell the tale.

"But this is unbelievable!" said their father, dressing as quickly as possible. "Simply unbelievable! Is Ned really down a secret passage, holding three spies at bay? And Ben has gone off with their motorboat? Am I dreaming?"

"No, Dad, you're not," said Alec. "It's all quite true. We kept everything a secret till tonight, because secrets are such fun. We didn't know that anything serious was up till tonight, really. Are you going to get help?"

"I certainly am," said his father. He went to the telephone downstairs and was soon on to the nearest military camp. He spoke to a most surprised commanding officer, who listened in growing amazement.

"So you must send a few men over as quickly as possible," said Father. "The children say there are three men in the caves – or rather, two men and one woman – but there may be more, of course, and more may arrive. We can't tell. Hurry, won't you?"

He put down the receiver of the telephone and turned to look at the waiting children. "Now let me see," he said thoughtfully. "I shall want one of you to take me to where Ned is, and I must leave someone behind to guide the soldiers down to the cove. They must be there to guard the entrance to the caves, so that if the spies try to escape by the beach, they will find they can't. Alec, you had better come with me. Frances and Hilary, you can go with Mother and the soldiers, when they come, and show them the way down the cliff and the entrance to the caves. Come along, Alec."

The two set off. Alec talked hard all the way, for there was a great deal to tell. His father listened in growing astonishment. Really, you never knew what children were doing half the time!

"I suppose your mother thought you were playing harmless games of smugglers," he said, "and all the time you were on the track of dangerous spies! Well, well, well!"

"We didn't really know they were spies till tonight," said Alec honestly. "It was all a game at first. Look, Dad – here's the hole. We have to slide down this rope."

"This really is a weird adventure," said his father,

and down the rope he went. Alec followed him.
Soon they were standing beside Uncle Ned, who
was still in the passage, his revolver in his hand.

"There's been a lot of excited talking," he said in
a low voice to his brother, "and I think they've
been trying to find a way out. But the tide is still
very high, and they daren't walk out on the sand
yet. If they don't know of this passage, they won't
try it, of course, but we'd better stay here in case
they do. When are the soldiers coming?"

"At once," said Father. "I've left the two girls
behind to guide them down to the cove. Then they
will hide and guard the entrance to the caves, that
is as soon as the tide goes down enough."

"Do the spies know you're here, Uncle Ned?"
asked Alec in a low voice.

"No," said his uncle. "They know someone has
gone off with their motorboat, but that's all they
know. What about creeping down to the end of the
passage to see if we can overhear anything? They
might drop a few secrets!"

The three of them crept down to the end of the
passage and leaned out over the hole that led down
to the space between the two caves. They could
hear the waves still washing up the narrow channel
in the long cave.

The two men and the woman were talking

angrily. "Who could have known we were here? Someone has given the game away! No one but ourselves and the other three knew what we were planning to do."

"Is there no other way out?" said a man's impatient voice, very deep and foreign. "Rondel, you know all these caves and passages – or so you said. How did the old smugglers get their goods away? There must have been a land path which they used."

"There was," said the other man. "There is a passage above this cave that leads on to the moors. But as far as I know it has been completely blocked by a roof-fall."

"As far as you know!" said the other man, in a scornful voice. "Haven't you found out? What do you suppose you are paid for, Rondel? Aren't you paid for letting us know any well-hidden caves on this coast? Where is this passage? Do you know?"

"Yes, I know," said Rondel. "It's above this one, and the entrance to it is just between this cave and the one we used for the motorboat. We have to climb up a little way. I've never been up it myself, because I heard it was blocked up by a roof-fall years ago. But we can try it and see."

"We'd better get back up the passage a bit," whispered Alec's father. "If they come up here, we may have trouble. Get on to that bit where the big rock juts out and the passage goes round it. We can get behind that and give them a scare. They'll shoot if they see us. I don't want to shoot if I can help it, for I've a feeling they will be more useful alive than dead!"

Very silently the three went back up the passage to where a rock jutted out and the way went round it. They crouched down behind the rock and waited, their torches switched off. Alec heard their breathing and it sounded very loud. But they had to breathe! He wondered if his father and uncle could hear his heart beating, because it seemed to make a very loud thump just then!

Meanwhile, the three spies were trying to find the entrance to the passage. Rondel had a powerful torch, and he soon found the hole that led to the ledge where the secret passage began.

"Here it is!" he said. "Look – we can easily get up there. I'll go first."

Alec heard a scrambling noise as the man climbed up. Then he pulled up the other two. They all switched on their torches and the dark passage was lit up brightly.

"It seems quite clear," said the other man. "I should think we could escape this way. You go ahead, Rondel. We'll follow. I can't see any sign of it being blocked up, I must say! This is a bit of luck."

They went on up the passage, talking. They went slowly, and Alec and the others could hear their footsteps and voices coming gradually nearer. Alec's heart beat painfully and he kept swallowing at a lump in his throat. The excitement was almost too much for him to bear.

The three spies came almost up to the jutting-out rock. And then they got the shock of their lives! Alec's father spoke in a loud stern voice that made Alec jump.

"Halt! Come another step, and we'll shoot!"

The spies halted at once in a panic. They switched off their torches.

"Who's there?" came Rondel's voice.

Nobody answered. The spies talked together in low voices and decided to go back the way they had come. They were not risking going round that rock! They didn't know how many people were there. It was plain that somebody knew of their plans and meant to capture them.

Alec heard the three making their way quietly back down the passage.

"Dad! I expect they think the tide will soon be going down and they hope to make their escape by way of the beach," whispered Alec. "I hope the soldiers will be there in time."

"Don't you worry about that!" said his father. "As soon as the tide washes off the beach, it will be full of soldiers."

"I wish I could be there," said Alec longingly. "I don't expect the spies will come up here again."

"Well, you can go and see what's happening if you like," said his father. "Your uncle and I will stay here – but you can see if the soldiers have arrived and if the girls are taking them down to the cove."

Alec was delighted. More excitement for him, after all! He went up the passage and swarmed up the rope out of the entrance-hole. He sped over the moor to the cottage. But no one was there. It was quite empty.

"I suppose the soldiers have arrived and Mother and the girls have taken them to the cove," thought Alec. "Yes, there are big wheel-marks in the road – a lorry has been here. Oh, there it is, in the shade of those trees over there. I'd better hurry or I'll miss the fun!"

Off he dashed to the cliff edge, and down the narrow, steep path. Where were the others? Waiting in silence down on the beach? Alec nearly fell down the steep path trying to hurry! What an exciting night!

10

The End of it All

Just as Alec was scrambling down the steep cliff, he heard the sound of a low voice from the top: "Is that you, Alec?"

Alec stopped. It was Ben's voice. "Ben!" he whispered in excitement. "Come on down. You're just in time. How did you get here?"

Ben scrambled down beside him. "I thought it was you," he said. "I saw you going over the edge of the cliff as I came up the lane. What's happened?"

Alec told him. Ben listened in excitement.

"So they know there's someone in the secret passage," he said. "They'll just have to try to escape by the beach then! Well, they'll be overpowered there, no doubt about that. I tied up the motor-boat by the jetty, Alec. It's a real beauty – small but very powerful. It's got a lovely engine. Then I raced back to see if I could be in at the end."

"Well, you're just in time," said Alec. "I'm going to hop down on to the beach now and see where the others are."

"Be careful," Ben warned him. "The soldiers won't know it's you, and may take a pot-shot at you." That scared Alec. He stopped before he jumped down on to the sand.

"Well, I think maybe we'd better stay here then," he said. "We can see anything that happens from here, can't we? Look, the tide is going down nicely now. Where do you suppose the others are, Ben?"

"I should think they're somewhere on the rocks that run round the cove," said Ben, looking carefully round. "Look, Alex, there's something shining just over there – see? I guess that's a gun. We can't see the man holding it but the moonlight just picks out a shiny bit of his gun."

"I hope the girls and Mother are safe," said Alec.

"I'm sure they are," said Ben. "I wonder what the spies are doing now. I guess they're waiting till the tide is low enough for them to come out."

At that very moment Rondel was looking out of the big cave to see if it was safe to try and escape over the beach. He was not going to try to go up the cliff path, for he felt sure there would be someone at the top. Their only hope lay in slipping round the corner of the cove and making their way up the cliff some way off. Rondel knew the coast by heart, and if he only had the chance he felt certain he could take the others to safety.

The tide was going down rapidly. The sand was very wet and shone in the moonlight. Now and again a big wave swept up the beach, but the power behind it was gone. It could not dash anyone against the rocks now. Rondel turned to his two companions and spoke to them in a low voice.

"Now's our chance. We shall have to try the beach while our enemies think the tide is still high. Take hold of Gretel's hand, Otto, in case a wave comes. Follow me. Keep as close to the cliff as possible in case there is a watcher above."

The three of them came silently out of the big cave. Its entrance lay in darkness and they looked like deep black shadows as they moved quietly to the left of the cave. They made their way round the rocks, stopping as a big wave came splashing up the smooth sand. It swept round their feet, but no higher. Then it ran back down the sand again to the sea, and the three moved on once more.

Then a voice rang out in the moonlight: "We have you covered! There is no escape this way! Hands up!"

Rondel had his revolver in his hand in a moment and guns glinted in the hands of the others, too. But they did not know where their enemies were. The rocks lay in black shadows, and no one could be seen.

"There are men all round this cove," said the voice. "You cannot escape. Put your hands up and surrender. Throw your revolvers down, please."

Rondel spoke to the others in a savage voice. He was in a fierce rage, for all his plans were ruined. It seemed as if he were urging the others to fight. But they were wiser than Rondel. The other man threw his revolver down on the sand and put his hands above his head. The woman did the same. They glinted there like large silver shells.

"Hands up, you!" commanded a voice. Rondel shouted something angry in a foreign language and then threw his gun savagely at the nearest rocks. It hit them and the trigger was jolted. The revolver went off with a loud explosion that echoed round and round the little cove and made everyone, Rondel as well, jump violently.

"Stand where you are," said a voice. And out from the shadow of the rocks came a soldier in the uniform of an officer. He walked up to the three spies and had a look at them. He felt them all over to see if there were any more weapons hidden about them. There were none.

He called to his men. "Come and take them."

Four men stepped out from the rocks around the cove. Alec and Ben leaped down on to the sand. Mother and the two girls came out from their hiding-place in a small cave. Ben ran up to the spies. He peered into the face of one of the men.

"I know who this is!" he cried. "It's Professor Rondel, who lived in Sea Cottage. I've seen him hundreds of times! He didn't have many friends – only two or three men who came to see him sometimes."

"Oh," said the officer, staring with interest at Ben. "Well, we'll be very pleased to know who the two or three men were. You'll be very useful to us, my boy. Now then – quick march! Up the cliff we go and into the lorry! The sooner we get these three into a safe place the better."

Alec's father and uncle appeared at that moment. They had heard the sound of the shot when Rondel's revolver struck the rock and went off, and they had come to see what was happening. Alec ran to them and told them.

"Good work!" said Father. "Three spies caught – and maybe the others they work with, too, if Ben can point them out. Good old Smuggler Ben!"

The three spies were put into the lorry and the driver climbed up behind the wheel. The officer saluted and took his place. Then the lorry rumbled off into the moonlit night. The four children watched it go, their eyes shining.

"This is the most thrilling night I've ever had in

my life," said Alec, with a sigh. "I don't suppose I'll ever have a more exciting one, however long I live. Gosh, my heart did beat fast when we were hiding in the cave. It hurt me."

"Same here," said Hilary. "Oh, Daddy – you didn't guess what you were in for, did you, when you came home yesterday?"

"I certainly didn't," said her father, putting his arm round the two girls and pushing them towards the house. "Come along – you'll all be tired out. It must be nearly dawn!"

"Back to Professor Rondel's own house!" said Alec. "Isn't it funny! He got all his information from his books – and we found some of it there, too. We'll show you if you like, Dad."

"Not tonight," said Father, firmly. "Tonight – or rather this morning, for it's morning now – you are going to bed, and to sleep. No more excitement, please! You will have plenty again tomorrow, for you'll have to go over to the police and to the military camp to tell all you know."

Well, that was an exciting piece of news, too. The children went indoors, Ben with them, for Mother said he had better share Alec's room for the rest of the night.

Soon all four children were in their beds, feeling certain they would never, never be able to go to sleep for one moment. But it wasn't more than two minutes before they were all sound asleep, as Mother saw when she peeped into the two bedrooms. She went to join Father and Uncle Ned.

"Well, I'd simply no idea what the children were doing," she told them. "I was very angry with them one night when they came home late because they were caught by the tide when they were exploring those caves. They kept their secret well."

"They're good kids," said Father, with a yawn. "Well, let's go to sleep, too. Ned, I hope you'll be able to drop off on the sofa again."

"I could drop off on the kitchen stove, I'm so tired!" said Ned.

Soon the whole household slept soundly, and did not wake even when the sun came slanting in at the windows. They were all tired out.

They had a late breakfast, and the children chattered nineteen to the dozen as they ate porridge and bacon and eggs. It all seemed amazingly wonderful to them now that it was over. They couldn't help feeling rather proud of themselves.

"I must go," said Ben, when he had finished an enormous breakfast. "My uncle is expecting me to go out fishing with him this morning.

He'll be angry because I'm late."

But before Ben could go, a messenger on a motorbike arrived, asking for the four children to go over to the police station at once. The police wanted to know the names of the men with whom Professor Rondel had made friends. This was very important, because unless they knew the names at once, the men might hear of Rondel's capture and fly out of the country.

So off went the four children, and spent a most exciting time telling and retelling their story from the very beginning. The inspector at the police station listened carefully, and when everything had been told, and notes taken, he leaned back and looked at the children, his eyes twinkling.

"Well, we have reason to be very grateful to you four smugglers," he said. "We shall probably catch the whole nest of spies operating in this part of the country. We suspected it, but we had no idea who the ringleader was. It was Rondel, of course. He was bringing men and women across from Ireland – spies, of course – and taking them about the country either to get information useful to the enemy, or to wreck valuable buildings. He was using the old smugglers' caves to hide his friends in. We shall comb the whole coast now."

"Can we help you?" asked Ben eagerly. "I know

most of the caves, sir. And we can show you Rondel's books, where all the old caves are described. He's got dozens of them."

"Good!" said the inspector. "Well, that's all for today. You will hear from us later. There will be a little reward given to you for services to your country!"

The children filed out, talking excitedly. A little reward! What could it be?

"Sometimes children are given watches as a reward," said Alec, thinking of a newspaper report he had read. "We might get a watch each."

"I hope we don't," said Hilary, "because I've already got one – though it doesn't keep very good time."

But the reward wasn't watches. It was something much bigger than that. Can you possibly guess what it was?

It was the little motorboat belonging to the spies! When the children heard the news, they could hardly believe their ears. But it was quite true. There lay the little motorboat, tied up to the jetty, and on board was a police officer with instructions to hand it over to the four children.

"Oh – thank you!" said Alec, hardly able to speak. "Thank you very much. Oh, Ben – oh, Ben – isn't it marvellous!"

It was marvellous! It was a beautiful little boat with a magnificent engine. It was called *Otto*.

"That won't do," said Hilary, looking at the name. "We'll have that painted out at once. What shall we call our boat? It must be a very good name – something that will remind us of our adventure!"

"I know – I know!" yelled Alec. "We'll call it *Smuggler Ben*, of course – and good old Ben shall be the captain, and we'll be his crew."

So *Smuggler Ben* the boat was called, and everyone agreed that it was a really good name. The children have a wonderful time in it. You should see them chug-chugging over the sea at top speed, the spray flying high in the air! Aren't they lucky!

THE BOY WHO WANTED A DOG

1

When Granny Came to Tea

"Hello, Granny!" said Donald, rushing in from afternoon school. "I hope you've come to tea!"

"Yes, I have!" said Granny. "And I've come to ask you a question, too. It's your birthday soon – what would you like me to give you?"

"He really doesn't deserve a birthday present," said his father, looking up from his paper. "His weekly reports from school haven't been good."

"Well, Dad – I'm not brainy like you," said Donald, going red. "I do try. I really do. But arithmetic beats me, I just can't do it. And I just hate trying to write essays and things. I can't seem to think of a thing to say!"

"You can work if you want to," said his mother, beginning to pour out the tea. "Look what your master said about your nature work – 'Best work in the whole form. Knows more about birds and animals than anyone.' Well, why can't you do well at writing and arithmetic!"

"They're not as interesting as nature," said Donald. "Now, when we have lessons about dogs and horses and squirrels and birds, I don't miss a word! And I write jolly good essays about them!"

"Did you get good marks today?" asked his father.

Donald shook his head and his father frowned. "I suppose you sat dreaming as usual!" he said.

"Well, geography was so dull this morning that I somehow couldn't keep my mind on it," said Donald. "It was all about things called peninsulas and isthmuses."

"And what were you keeping your mind on – if it happened to be working?" asked his father.

"Well . . . I was thinking about a horse I saw when I was going to school this morning," said Donald, honestly.

"But why think of a horse in your geography lesson?" said his mother.

"Well, Mum, it was a nice old horse, and doing its best to pull a heavy cart," said Donald. "And I couldn't help noticing that it had a dreadful sore place on its side, which was being rubbed by the harness. And oh, Mum, instead of being sorry for the horse, the man was hitting it!"

"And so you thought of the horse all through your geography lesson?" said Granny, gently.

"Well, I couldn't help it," said Donald. "I kept wondering if the man would put something on the sore place, when he got the horse home. I kept thinking what I would do if it were my horse. Granny, people who keep animals should be kind to them, and notice when they are ill or hurt, shouldn't they?"

"Of course they should," said Granny. "Well, don't worry about the horse any more. I'm sure the man has tended it by now. Let's talk of something happier. What would you like for your birthday?"

"Oh Granny – there's something I want more than anything else in the world!" said Donald, his eyes shining.

"Well, if it's not too expensive and is possible to get, you shall have it!" said Granny. "What is it?"

"A puppy!" said Donald, in an excited voice. "A puppy of my very own! I can make him a kennel myself. I'm good with my hands, you know!"

"No, Donald!" said his mother, at once. "I will not have a dirty little puppy messing about the house, chewing the mats to pieces, rushing about tripping everyone up, and—"

"He wouldn't! He wouldn't!" said Donald. "I'd train him well. He'd walk at my heels. He could sleep in my bedroom on a rug. He could—"

"Sleep in your room! Certainly not!" said his mother quite shocked. "No, Granny – not a puppy, please. Donald's bad enough already, the things he brings home; caterpillars, a hedgehog – ugh, the prickly thing – a stray cat that smelled dreadful and stole the fish out of the larder and . . ."

"Oh Mum – I wouldn't bring anything into the house if only you'd let me have a puppy!" said Donald. "It's the thing I want most in the world. A puppy of my very own! Granny, please, please give me one."

"No," said his father. "You don't deserve a puppy while your schoolwork is so bad. Sorry, Granny. You'll have to give him something else."

Granny looked sad. "Well, Donald – I'll give you some books about animals," she said. "Perhaps your father will let you have a puppy when you get a good school report."

"I never will," said poor Donald. "I'm not nearly as clever as the other boys, except with my hands. I'm making you a little footstool, Granny, for your birthday, I'm carving a pattern all round it – and the woodwork master said that even he couldn't have done it better. I'm good with my hands."

"You've something else that is good too," said Granny. "You've a good heart, Donald, and a kind one. Well, if you can't have a puppy for your birthday, you must come with me to the bookshop and choose some really lovely books. Would you like one about dogs – and another about horses, or cats?"

"Yes. I'd like those very much," said Donald. "But oh, how I'd love a puppy."

"Let's change the subject," said his father. "What about tea? I see some of Mother's chocolate cakes on the table, Granny. Donald, forget this puppy business, please, and take a chair to the table for Granny."

So there they all were, sitting at the tea table, eating sandwiches, chocolate cakes and biscuits. Donald wasn't talking very much. He was thinking hard – dreaming, as his teacher would say.

"Where would I keep the puppy if I had one?" he thought. "Let me see – I could make a little kennel, and put it in my own bit of garden. How pleased the puppy would be to see me each morning. What should I call him – Buster? Scamper? Wags? Barker? No, he mustn't bark, Mum would be cross. I'll teach him to . . ."

"Look! Donald's dreaming again!" said his mother. "Wake up, Donald! Pass Granny the cakes! I wonder what you're dreaming about now!"

Granny knew! She smiled at him across the table. Dear Donald! Why couldn't she give him the puppy that he so much wanted?

2

All Because of a Kitten

Two days later Donald had quite an adventure! It was all because of a kitten. He was walking home from school, swinging his school-bag, and saying "Hello" to all the dogs he met, when he suddenly saw a kitten run out of a front gate. It was a very small one, quite black, fluffy and round-eyed.

"I'll have to take that kitten back into its house, or it will be run over!" thought Donald, and began to run. But someone else had seen it too – the dog across the road.

Across the road sped the dog, barking. The kitten was terrified and tried to run up a nearby tree, but it wasn't in time to escape the dog, who stood with his forepaws on the trunk of the tree, snapping at the kitten's tail and barking.

"Stop it! Get down!" shouted Donald, racing up. "Leave the kitten alone!"

The dog raced off. Donald looked at the terrified kitten, clinging to the tree-trunk. Was it hurt?

He picked it gently off the tree and looked at it. "You poor little thing – the dog has bitten your tail. It's bleeding. Whatever can I do? I'll just take you into the house nearby and see if you belong there."

But no – the woman there shook her head. "It's not our kitten. I don't know who it belongs to. It's been around for some time and nobody really wants it. That's why it's so thin, poor mite."

"What a shame!" said Donald, stroking the frightened little thing. It cuddled closer to him, digging its tiny claws into his coat, holding on tightly. It gave a very small mew.

"Well, I'd better take it home," thought Donald. "I can't possibly leave it in the street. That dog would kill it if he caught it! But whatever will Mum say? She doesn't like cats."

He tucked it gently under his coat and walked home, thinking hard. What about that old tumbledown shed at the bottom of the garden? He could put a box there with an old piece of cloth in it for the kitten, and somehow he could manage to make the door shut so that it would be safe.

"You see, your tail is badly bitten," he said to the kitten, whose head was now peeping out of his coat. "You can't go running about with such a hurt tail. I'll have to get some ointment and a bandage."

Donald thought he had better not take the kitten into the house. There might be a fuss. So he took the little thing straight to the old shed at the bottom of the garden. He saw an old sack there and put it into a box. Then he put the kitten there, and stroked it, talking in the special voice he kept for animals – low and kind and comforting. The kitten gave a little purr.

"Ah – so you can purr, you poor little thing! I shouldn't have thought there was a purr left in you, after your fright this morning!" said Donald. "Now I'm going to find some ointment and a bandage – and some milk perhaps!"

He shut the shed door carefully, and put a big stone across the place where there was a hole at the bottom. Then he went down to the house. "Is that you, Donald?" called his mother. "Lunch will be ready in ten minutes."

Ten minutes! Good! There would be time to find what he wanted and go quickly back to the shed. He ran into the kitchen, which was empty – his mother was upstairs. Quickly he went to the cupboard where medicines and ointments were kept, and took out a small pot and a piece of lint.

Then he took an old saucer, went to the fridge, and poured some milk into it. He tiptoed out of the kitchen door into the garden, thankful that no one had seen him.

Up to the old shed he went. The kitten was lying peacefully in the box, licking her bitten tail. "I wouldn't use your rough little tongue on that sore place," said Donald. "Let me put some ointment on it. It will feel better then. Perhaps it's a good thing, really, you've licked it – it's your way of washing the hurt place clean, I suppose. Now, keep still, I won't hurt you!"

And very gently, he took the kitten on to his knee and stroked it. It began to purr. Donald dipped his finger into the ointment and rubbed it gently over the bitten place. The kitten gave a sudden yowl of pain and almost leaped off his knee!

"Sorry!" said Donald, stroking it. "Now keep still while I wrap this bit of lint round your tail, and tie it in place."

The kitten liked Donald's soft, gentle voice. It lay still once more, and let the boy put on the piece of lint – but when he tied it in place, it yowled again, and this time managed to jump right off his knee to the ground!

Donald had put the saucer of milk down on the floor when he had come to the shed, and the kitten suddenly saw it. It ran to it in surprise and began to lap eagerly, forgetting all about its hurt tail.

The boy was delighted. He had bound up the bitten tail, and had given the kitten milk – the two things he had come to do. He bent down and stroked the soft little head.

"Now you keep quiet here, in your box," he said. "I'll come and see you as often as I can."

He opened the door while the kitten was still lapping its milk, shut it, and went up the garden. He was happy. He liked thinking about the tiny creature down in the shed. It was his now. It was a shame that nobody had wanted it or cared for it. What a pity his mother didn't like cats! If she had loved it, it could have had such a nice home.

"I'll have to find a home for it," he thought. "I'll get its tail better first, and then see if I can find someone who would like to have it!"

The kitten drank a little more milk, climbed back into its box, sniffed at the lint round its tail, and went sound asleep, safe for the night!

3

A Job for Donald

It was not until the next morning that Donald found a chance to slip down to the shed to see the kitten. He took some more milk with him, and a few scraps.

"It will be so hungry!" he thought. "What a good thing I left it some milk!"

But the milk had hardly been touched, and the kitten was lying very still in its box. It gave a faint mew when Donald bent over it, as if to say, "Here's that kind boy again!"

"You don't look well, little kitten," said Donald surprised. "What's the matter? You haven't drunk the milk I left!"

He knew what the matter was when he saw the kitten's tail. It was very swollen, and the tiny creature had torn off the bandage with its teeth! It was in pain, and looked up at the boy as if to say "Please help me!"

"Oh dear – something has gone wrong with your poor little tail!" said Donald. "Perhaps the wound has gone bad, like my finger did when I cut it on a tin. Now what am I to do with you?"

The kitten lay quite still, looking up at Donald. "I can't take you indoors," said the boy. "My mother doesn't like cats. I think I'd better take you to the vet. You needn't be frightened. He's an animal doctor, and he loves little things like you. He'll make your tail better, really he will!"

"Mew-ew!" the kitten said faintly, glad to see this boy with the kind voice and gentle hands. It cried out when he lifted it up and put it under his coat.

"Did I hurt your poor tail?" said Donald. "I couldn't help it. If we go quickly I'll have time to take you to the vet's as soon as he's there. It's a good thing it's Saturday, else I would have had to go to school."

There were already three people in the vet's surgery when Donald arrived – a man with a dog, whose paw was bandaged; a women with a parrot that had a drooping wing; and a small girl with a pet mouse in a box. One by one they were called into the surgery, and at last it was Donald's turn.

The vet was a big man with big hands – hands that were amazingly gentle and deft. He saw at once that the kitten's tail was in a very bad state.

"It was bitten by a dog," said Donald. "I did my best – put ointment on and bound it up."

"You did well, Donald," said the vet. "Poor mite! I'm afraid it will have to lose half its tail. It's been bitten too badly to save. But I don't expect it will worry overmuch at having a short tail!"

"Perhaps the other cats will think it's a Manx cat," said Donald. "Manx cats have short tails, don't they?"

The vet smiled. "Yes. Now you'll have to leave the kitten with me, and I must deal with its tail. It will be quite all right. It won't be unhappy here."

Donald liked the vet very much. His big hands held the kitten very gently, and the little thing began to purr.

"Do all animals like you, sir?" he asked.

"Oh yes — animals always know those who are their friends," he said. "That kitten knows you are its friend. It will let you handle it without fear. I'll keep it for a week, then you can have it back."

"Er — how much will your bill be?" asked Donald.

"Oh, you needn't worry about that, Donald!" said the vet. "I'll send the bill to your father."

"But, sir, my father and mother don't know about the kitten," said Donald. "You see, I kept it in our shed. It isn't mine, it's a stray. I rescued it from the dog. My mother doesn't like animals very much — especially cats. I'd like to pay your bill myself.

The only thing is, I haven't much money just at present."

"Well now, would you like to earn a little, by helping me?" said the vet. "You could pay off the bill that way! My kennel-maid is away for a few days – she looks after the dogs here for me, feeds them and brushes them. You could do that, couldn't you, for a few evenings?"

"Oh yes! Yes, I could," said Donald, really delighted. "I'd love to. But would you trust me to do the job properly? We've never had a dog at home. But I love dogs, I really do."

"I'd trust any boy with any animal here, if he handled a kitten as gently as you do," said the vet. "It isn't everyone who has the gift of understanding animals, you know. You're lucky!"

"My granny says that anyone who loves animals understands them," said Donald.

"She's right," said the vet. "Now look – I've more patients waiting for me, as you saw. Leave the kitten in that basket. I'll attend to it as soon as I can. Come back tonight at half past five, and I'll introduce you to the dogs. Right?"

"Yes, sir," said Donald, joyfully, and put the kitten gently into the basket on the floor. Then out he went, very happy.

The kitten would be all right now. He could pay

the bill by taking the job the vet offered him – and what a job! Seeing to dogs, feeding them, perhaps taking them for walks! But wait a bit – what would his parents say?

He told his father first. "Daddy, the vet wants a boy to help him a bit while his kennel-maid is away," said Donald. "I thought I'd take the job – it's in the evenings – and earn a bit of money. You're always saying that boys are lazy nowadays, not like when you were young, and went out and earned money even while you were at school."

"Well! I didn't think you had it in you to take a job like that!" said his father. "I'm pleased. So long as you don't neglect your homework, you can help the vet. Well, well – and I thought you were such a lazy young monkey!"

Donald was delighted. He could hardly wait for the evening to come! Looking after dogs! Would they like him? Would he be able to manage them? Well – he would soon know!

4

Donald Goes to Work!

Donald could hardly wait for the evening to come. He did his usual Saturday jobs – ran errands for his mother, cleaned his father's bicycle and his own, and weeded a corner of the garden.

Then his mother called him. "What's this I hear from your father about your working for the vet? You know he's an animal doctor? You'll come home all smelly and dirty!"

"I shan't, Mum," said Donald, in alarm. "Goodness me, you should see the vet's place – as clean as our own! Anyway, Dad says it will be good for me."

"Well, if you do come home smelling of those animals up at the vet's place, you'll have to give up the job," said his mother. "Fancy wanting to go and work with animals! I'm surprised at your father letting you!"

Donald kept out of his mother's way all day, really afraid that she would forbid him to go up to the vet's house that evening. He put on his very oldest clothes and, when at last the clock said a quarter past five, off he went at top speed on his bicycle. His first job! And with dogs too! How lucky he was!

He arrived at the vet's, put his bicycle in a shed and went to find the kennels. The vet was there, attending to a dog with a crushed paw.

"Ah – you're here already, Donald!" he said. "Good. You're early, so you can give me a hand with this poor old fellow. He's had such a shock that he's scared stiff. I want to calm him down before I do anything."

"What happened?" asked Donald, shocked to see the poor, misshapen front paw of the trembling dog.

"It was caught in a door," said the vet. "Apparently the wind slammed the door shut, and he couldn't get his paw away in time. He's a nervy dog. Do you think you can hold him still while I examine the paw?"

"I don't know. I'll try," said Donald. He stroked the dog and spoke to it in his "special" voice – the one he used for animals. "Poor old boy – never mind – you'll soon be able to walk on that paw. Poor old boy, then, poor old boy."

The dog turned to him, pricked its ears, and listened. Then it licked Donald on the cheek, and gave a little whine of pain.

"Go on talking to him," said the vet. "Don't stop. He's listening to you. He won't mind about me if you take his attention."

So Donald went on talking and stroking, and the dog listened, trying to get as close to the boy as he could. This boy was a comforting boy. This boy had a lovely, clean, boy-smell. He was worth listening to!

The dog gave a little whine now and again as the vet worked on his hurt paw. Soon the vet spoke to him. "Nearly over now, old thing. I'm putting a

plaster on, so don't be afraid. You'll be able to walk all right, your foot will be protected. Nearly over now."

The dog gave a huge sigh and laid his head on Donald's shoulder. Donald was so happy to feel it there that he could hardly speak to the dog for a moment. He found himself repeating what the vet had said. "Nearly over now, old thing, nearly over now."

"Well – that's it," said the vet, standing up. "Come on, old boy, to your kennel, now, and a nice long sleep."

The dog followed him, limping. Donald went too. The dog licked his hand every now and again, as if thanking him. The vet put him into a roomy kennel with straw on the floor, and shut the door. "Goodnight, old boy!" called Donald, and from the kennel came a short bark – "Woof-woof!"

"He'll be all right," said the vet. "You did well to hold him, Donald, a big dog like that. You have a good voice for animals, too. Now, here are the dogs I want you to brush, and to give fresh water to. Clean up any kennels that need it. You'll find fresh straw over there if necessary."

Donald had never had such an interesting evening in all his life. There were five dogs in the kennels, each in a separate one – and all the dogs were different! He looked at them carefully.

"An Alsatian . . . a Labrador – goodness, he's fat – and a corgi with stubby little legs. He looks very intelligent. What's this dog, over in the kennel corner . . . a little black poodle – what a pet! And this last one, well, goodness knows what it is, a real mixture. A bit of terrier, a bit of a spaniel, and a bit of something else!"

The dogs barked with joy when the boy came to them. They loved company of any sort and were longing for a walk.

"Three of them are here because their owners are away from home," said the vet. "The corgi has a bad ear. The little mongrel ate something he shouldn't and nearly poisoned himself, but he's feeling better now. You won't be scared of going into their kennels, will you? Their bark is worse than their bite!"

"Oh no, sir, I'm not scared!" said Donald. "Shall I take them for a walk when I've finished?"

"Not tonight – we're a bit late," said the vet. "I'll take them out myself, last thing. You get on with the brushing."

He left Donald alone. The boy was too happy for words. He had five dogs to see to – five! And what was more, they all seemed as pleased to see him, as he was to see them!

"Hello, all of you!" he said. "I'm just going to fetch a can of fresh water for you. Then I'll clean out your kennels, put down fresh straw, and have a word with each of you. Shan't be long."

And off he went, whistling loudly, to the tap he saw in the distance. He filled a large can with water, and went back to the dogs. They were whining and barking now, the bigger ones standing with their paws on the top of their gates.

"I like you all very much," said Donald, in his "special" voice. "I hope you like me too."

"Woof-woof, WUFF, whine-whine, WOOF-WOOF!" Yes, they certainly liked Donald, no doubt about that.

5

A Wonderful Evening

Donald had a wonderful evening with the five dogs. He went first into the Labrador's kennel – it was rather like a small shed with a half-door or gate at the front, to get in by, fastened with a latch on the outer side.

The Labrador was a big dog, a lovely golden colour. He stared at Donald in silence as the boy went in. "Hello!" said Donald. "How are you? Sorry I don't know your name. I've brought you some fresh water, and I'll sweep out your kennel and give you some fresh straw. Will you like that?"

The Labrador lumbered over to the boy and sniffed his legs and hands. Then he wagged his tail slowly. Donald patted him. "Are you homesick?" he said. "Poor old boy! Do you miss your master?"

At the word "master" the Labrador pricked up his ears and gave a little whine. Donald emptied out the water-bowl, wiped it round with a cloth he had found by the tap, and poured in fresh water. The Labrador lapped it eagerly. He didn't like stale water – this was lovely and cold and fresh! He sniffed at Donald again, decided that he liked him, and licked his bare hand.

Donald patted him, delighted. "Sorry I can't stay long with you," he said. "I've the other dogs to see to. But I'll be back to give you a brush when I've finished."

He went to the Alsatian's kennel next. This too was a big one, almost a shed. "Hello!" said Donald. "My word, you've got a big water-bowl. You must be a thirsty dog! Hey, don't drink out of the can, greedy! That's right – you've plenty in your bowl! I'll come back again soon and brush you."

The Alsatian stopped drinking and went to his gate with Donald, hoping to get out and have a run. "No, old boy," said Donald, firmly. "You'll have to wait for your walk till the vet takes you out tonight. Hey, let me get out of the gate!"

He went to the poodle next, a dear little woolly-coated thing that danced about on tiptoe as soon as the boy came into her kennel. She licked Donald everywhere she could.

"I shall have to bring a towel with me when I come to see you," said Donald. "You really have a very wet tongue. Now – drink your water. I'll be back again in a minute!"

The other two dogs, the corgi and the mongrel, were not feeling very well, especially the corgi, whose ear was hurting him. They wagged their tails and whined when Donald went in to them. The mongrel was very thirsty and drank all his water at once. Donald patted him.

"You're thin," he said. "And you look sad. I'll bring you some more water when I come in to clean your kennel."

The mongrel pressed himself against the boy's legs, grateful for attention and kindness. He whined when Donald went out. That was a nice boy, he thought. He wished he could spend the night with him. He would cuddle up to him and perhaps he would feel better then!

The next thing was to clean out the kennels, and put in fresh straw. Once more the dogs were delighted when Donald appeared, and gave him loud and welcoming barks.

The vet, at work in his surgery, looked out of the window, pleased. The dogs sounded happy. That boy had made friends with them already. Ah, there he was, carrying a bundle of straw!

Donald cleaned out each kennel and put down fresh straw, and the five dogs nuzzled him and whined lovingly while he was in their kennels. He talked to them all the time, and they loved that. They listened with ears pricked, and gave little wuffs in answer. They gambolled round him, and licked his hand whenever they could. Donald had never felt so happy in all his life.

He had to brush each dog after he had cleaned the kennels, and this was the nicest job of all. The dogs really loved feeling the firm brushing with the hard-bristled brush. Each dog had his own brush, with his name on it so, to the dogs' delight, Donald suddenly knew their names and called them by them!

When he had finished his evening's work, he patted each dog and said goodnight. All five dogs watched him go, giving little barks as if to say, "Come back tomorrow! Do come back!"

"I'll be back!" called Donald, and went up to the surgery to report that he had finished. The vet clapped him on the shoulder and smiled.

"I've never heard the dogs so happy. Well done. Tomorrow is Sunday. Will you be able to come?"

"Oh yes – not in the morning, but I could come in the afternoon and evening, if you've enough jobs for me, sir!" said Donald. "I'll be glad to earn enough money to pay off the bill for the kitten! Could I see the kitten, sir? Is its tail better?"

"Getting on nicely," said the vet. "I've got it in the next room. Come and see it."

So into the next room they went, and there, in a neat little cage, lying on a warm rug, was the

kitten. It mewed with delight when it saw Donald, and stood up, pressing its nose against the cage.

"It only has half a tail now," said the boy sadly. "Poor little thing. Is it in pain still?"

"Oh no – hardly at all," said the vet. "But I must keep it quiet until the wound has healed."

"What will happen to it?" asked Donald. "Nobody will want a kitten with only half a tail, will they? I wish my mother would let me keep it."

"Don't worry about that," said the vet. "We'll find a kind home for it. You've done a good evening's work. Come along tomorrow, and you can take the dogs for a walk. I really think I can trust you with the whole lot!"

Donald sped home in delight. As soon as he arrived there, he rushed upstairs, ran a bath for himself, and then put on clean clothes. "Now Mum won't smell a doggy smell at all!" he thought. "I just smell of nice clean soap! But oh, I think a doggy smell is lovely! I can't wait till tomorrow, I really can't!"

6

Sunday Afternoon

Donald was very hungry for his supper. He had really worked hard that evening. His mother was surprised to see the amount of bread and butter that he ate with his boiled egg.

"What's made you so hungry?" she asked. "Oh, of course – you've been helping the vet, haven't you? What did you do?"

"I cleaned out the dog kennels – five of them," said Donald. "And I—"

"Cleaned out dog kennels! Whatever next?" said his mother, quite horrified.

"Well, I emptied the water-bowls and put in fresh water – and I brushed an Alsatian called Prince, a Labrador, a corgi, a poodle and a mongrel!" said Donald. "May I have some more bread and butter, please?"

His father began to laugh. "Boil him another egg, bless him," he said. "He's worked harder at the vet's this evening than he ever does at school. It's something to know that he can work well, even if it's just with dogs, and not with books."

"Well, these dogs are jolly interesting!" said Donald. "Dad, you should have seen how they all came round me – as if they'd known me for years!"

"That's all very well," said his mother, "but I do hope you won't forget your weekend homework in your excitement over these dogs."

"Gracious! Homework! Oh blow it, I'd forgotten all about it!" said Donald, in dismay. "It's those awful decimal sums again. I wish I could do sums about dogs – I'd soon do those! And I've an essay to write about some island or other – dull as ditchwater. Now, an essay about dogs – I could write pages!"

"Just forget about dogs for a bit and finish your supper," said his mother. "Then you really must do a little homework."

"I'm tired now. I'd get all my sums wrong," said Donald, yawning. "I'll do it tomorrow morning, before we go to church. I'm going to the vet's again in the afternoon and evening."

"My word – you are keen on your new job!" said his father. "I'm pleased about that. But I shall stop you going if your schoolwork suffers, remember."

Poor Donald! He really was tired that evening after his work with the dogs. He couldn't do his sums properly. His head nodded forward and he fell asleep. When he awoke he put away his undone work and went to bed, afraid that his parents would come in and find his homework still not done.

"I'll have time in the morning!" he thought. "I'll set my alarm clock and wake early. My mind is nice and clear then!"

So, when his alarm went at seven, he leaped out of bed and tackled his sums. Yes – they were easier to do first thing in the morning. But oh, that essay! He'd do that after breakfast. But after breakfast his mother wanted him to do some jobs for her and then he had to get ready to go to church. That silly essay! What was the sense of writing about something he wasn't at all interested in? If only he could write about those five dogs! Goodness, he would be able to fill pages and pages!

He had told the vet that he would be at the surgery at half past two. That left him just twenty minutes after Sunday lunch to do the essay! He took his pen and wrote at top speed, so that his writing was bad and his spelling poor, for he had no time to look up any words in the dictionary.

He looked at the rather smudgy pages when he had finished. His teacher would not be pleased. But he really hadn't time to do it all over again.

Maybe he could wake up early next morning and rewrite it!

Donald changed quickly into his old clothes and rushed out to get his bicycle. Then away he went, pedalling fast, glad that no one had stopped him, and asked him to do a job of some sort!

The boy had a wonderful afternoon. The vet took him into an airy little building where he kept birds that had been hurt, or were ill – and budgerigars that he bred himself for sale. Donald was enchanted with the little budgies. The vet let them out of their great cage, and they flew gaily round Donald's head, came to rest on his shoulder or his hand – and one even sat on his ear!

"Oh, how I'd love to breed budgies like these!" he said. "How I'd like a pair for my own!"

"Good afternoon," said a voice suddenly, almost in Donald's ear. "How are you, how are you, how are you?"

Donald looked round in surprise and then he laughed. "Oh – it's the parrot talking!" he said. "A lovely white cockatoo! Is he hurt, or something?"

"No. I'm just keeping him for a time because his owner is ill," said the vet. "He's a wonderful talker!"

"Shut the door! Do shut the door!" said the cockatoo, and Donald obediently went to the door!

242

The vet laughed. "Don't shut it! It's just something he knows how to say – one of the scores of things he's always repeating!"

The cockatoo cleared its throat exactly like Donald's father did. Then it spoke again, in a very cross voice. "Sit down! Stand up! Go to bed!"

Donald began to laugh – and the cockatoo laughed too – such a human laugh that the boy was really astonished. Then the vet took him to a shed where he kept any cats that needed his help. The little kitten was there too, curled up asleep, its short tail still bandaged. It looked very happy and contented. There were four big cats there also, one with a bandaged head, one with a leg in plaster.

"All my patients," said the vet, fondling one of them. "Cats are more difficult to treat than dogs, not so trusting. Mind that one – she's in pain at the moment, and might scratch you!"

But before the vet had even finished his sentence, Donald was stroking the cat, and talking to it in his "special" voice. It began to purr loudly, and put down its head for him to scratch its neck.

The vet was amazed. "Why, that cat will hardly let even me touch it!" he said. "Look, I need to change its bandage now – see if you can hold the cat quiet for me, will you? It fought me like a little fury this morning. Will you risk it? You may be well and truly scratched!"

"I'll risk it," said Donald, happily. "I love cats and kittens. Show me what to do, sir – how to hold her. Hark at her purring! She won't scratch me!"

But cats are different from dogs, and Donald knew that if he went home with his face scratched and torn, he wouldn't be allowed to go and help the vet again.

7

Donald is Very Busy

"What's the matter with the cat?" asked Donald, as he went on fondling the nervous animal.

"Its hind legs somehow got caught in a trap," said the vet. "One has mended well, but the other is badly torn and won't heal. So I have to paint the leg with some lotion that stings – and this the cat can't bear!"

"How did you manage to hold the cat and deal with its leg at the same time?" asked Donald, as the cat began to stiffen itself in fright. "Did the kennel-maid hold it for you when she was here?"

"Oh no, she was frightened of the cat," said the vet. "It's half-wild, anyhow – lives in the woods. The keeper brought it to me. It's a lovely cat, really, half Persian. Now, can you hold it, I'll show you how to."

Gently the vet took the cat and showed the boy how to hold it for him. The cat suddenly spat at him and tried to leap away, her claws out. But the vet's hold was firm and kind.

"I see, I see exactly," said Donald. "Poor old

puss, then. Don't be scared. We're your friends, you know. Poor old puss."

"Go on talking to the cat," said the vet. "It's listening to you just like that hurt dog did. You've a wonderful voice for animals. Many children have, if only they knew it – it's a low, kind, soothing voice that goes on and on and animals can't help listening. Go on talking to the cat, Donald. It's quieter already."

The cat struggled a little as Donald held her, talking smoothly and quietly in his special voice. Soon she lay limp in his hold, and let the vet do what he pleased with her bad leg. She gave a loud yowl once when the lotion suddenly stung, but that was all.

Soon the bandage was on again, and the cat lay quietly in Donald's arms, purring. "Shall I hold her for a bit?" said the boy. "She sort of wants comforting, I think."

The vet looked at the boy holding the wounded cat. "You know, son, you should be a vet yourself when you grow up!" he said. "You could do anything with animals! They trust you. How'd you like to be an animal-doctor?"

"I'd like it more than anything in the world!" said Donald. "I love animals so much – and they love me! They do, really. I've never had a real pet of my own – my parents aren't fond of animals – so I've always had to make do with caterpillars and a hedgehog or two, and once a little wild mouse . . ."

"And I don't suppose you were allowed to take them into the house, were you?" said the vet. "Well, some people like animals and everything to do with nature – and some don't. We're the lucky ones, you and I, aren't we?"

"Yes. We are," said Donald, carrying the cat back to its cage. "It's not much good my thinking of being an animal-doctor, though. I think I've got to go into my father's business and be an architect. And the awful thing is, I'm no good at figures or drawing or any of the things that architects have to do. I shall be a very, very bad architect and hate every minute. And I shall keep dozens of stray animals in my backyard, just to make up for it!"

The vet laughed. "If you want a thing badly enough, you'll get it," he said. "You'll be a vet one day, and be as happy as the day is long! Now to work again!"

Donald spent a very happy Sunday at the vet's. He helped him with more of the animals, he cleaned out the birds' cages and, best of all, he took all the five dogs for a long, long walk!

The vet telephoned his parents to ask them if

Donald could stay to tea with him, so he didn't need to rush home at half past four. He went to fetch the dogs, calling "Who's for a walk, a walk, a WALK!" They all began to bark in delight, and the Alsatian did his best to jump right over the top of his high kennel-gate!

"Take them on the hills," said the vet. "There will be few people there, and you can let them loose for a good run. Whistle them when you want them to come to you. Can you whistle, by the way?"

Donald promptly whistled so long, loudly and clearly that the vet jumped and all the dogs in the kennels began to bark in excitement!

"Watch out for the corgi when you're on the hills," said the vet. "He may not be able to keep up with the others, on his short legs. And don't lose the mongrel down a rabbit-hole – he's a terror for rabbits."

Donald set off happily, with the five dogs gambolling round him. They might have known him for years! Once on the hills they galloped about in joy. The mongrel promptly went halfway down a rabbit-hole, and Donald had to pull him out!

A man came walking down the hill towards them. Prince, the Alsatian, immediately went to

sniff at him, and the man shouted at him "Go away!" and struck out with his stick. The big Alsatian growled at once, showing all his strong white teeth.

"Call your dog off!" yelled the angry man to Donald and the boy suddenly stopped in astonishment. Goodness – it was Mr Fairly, his schoolteacher. He whistled to the Alsatian and the dog returned to him at once, and so did the other four! They all ran to him at top speed and milled round him in delight, whining for a pat.

Mr Fairly was astounded to see Donald – the dunce of the maths class – with five gambolling dogs! "What in the world are you doing with this army of dogs!" he yelled. "That Alsatian's dangerous!"

"He's all right, sir!" yelled back Donald, quite pleased to have seen his fierce maths master scared of a dog. "I'm taking them all for a walk. Heel, boys, heel!"

And, to the master's astonishment, every dog obediently rushed to Donald's heels, and walked behind as meekly as schoolchildren. Well, well – the boy might not be able to do sums but he could manage dogs all right! What a very surprising thing! There must be more in that boy than Mr Fairly had ever imagined!

8

Donald Gets into Trouble

In the week, Donald could only manage to go to the vet's in the evenings and how he looked forward to the time after tea when he could slip off to the kennels and see to the dogs. They welcomed him with barks that could surely be heard half a mile away!

But poor Donald had a shock when Wednesday arrived, and the essays of the weekend came up for correction. He had handed in his smudgy, hastily written one, ashamed of it, but not having had enough time to do it again.

Mr Fairly, his form master, had the piles of essays in front of him, and dealt with the good ones first, awarding marks. Then he looked sternly at Donald, and waved an exercise book at him – Donald's own book!

"This essay must be written all over again!" he said. "In fact, I'm almost inclined to say it should be written out three times. The spelling! The handwriting! The smudges! Donald, you should be in the lowest form, not this one! I am really ashamed to have a boy like you in my class."

"I'm sorry, sir. I – well – I had rather a lot to do in the weekend," said poor Donald.

"Ha yes – taking out dogs for a walk on the hills, I suppose!" said Mr Fairly. "Well, I shall ask your parents if they will please see that your homework is done – and done well – before you go racing off with the most peculiar collection of dogs that I have ever seen!"

"Oh please, sir, don't complain to my parents!" said Donald. "I'll rewrite the essay, sir. I'll – I'll write it out three times if you like!"

"Very well. Rewrite your essay three times tonight, and hand it in tomorrow," said Mr Fairly. "I fear, Donald, that that will mean five dogs will have to do without your company after tea!"

"The mean fellow!" thought Donald, angrily. "He must know I am taking the vet's dogs walking after tea and that's about the worst punishment he could give me – making me sit indoors, writing essays when he knows I love walking the dogs!"

But there was nothing to be done about it. Donald had to tell the vet he wouldn't be up after tea that day.

"Bad luck," said the vet, kindly. "The dogs will miss you. Never mind. Just come when you can. I'll manage."

Donald sat down after tea to rewrite his essay. Blow, bother, blow! What a waste of a lovely evening! Would the dogs miss him? Would they be looking out for him? What a pity he couldn't write about them, instead of rewriting his stupid essay!

His mother was astonished to find him in his bedroom, writing so busily. "I thought you would be up at the vet's," she said. "Are you doing extra homework, or something?"

"Well – sort of," said Donald. His mother looked closely at what he was doing and frowned.

"Oh Donald! You're rewriting an essay! And no wonder! What a mess you made of it – however could you give in work like that? I suppose you wrote it in a hurry because you give up so much time to helping the vet."

"The weekend was so busy," said Donald, desperately. "I just had to hurry over my essay."

"Well, you know what Daddy said – you can only go to help the vet if your schoolwork is good," said his mother. "I'm afraid you can't go there any more."

Donald stared at his mother, his heart going down into his boots. Not go any more? Not see those lovely dogs – and help with the cats and the birds? Not be with the vet again, the man he admired so much?

"I must go to the vet's," he said. "He's going to pay me for my work. I want the money for something."

"What for?" asked his mother, astonished.

Donald looked away. How could he tell her that he had taken that little kitten to the vet's to be healed and looked after, so that he might perhaps have it for his own pet, hidden away somewhere? How could he tell her that what he earned at the vet's was to pay for the kitten's treatment? She didn't like cats. So how could she understand what he felt for the tiny kitten that had been chased and bitten by a dog?

But it was all no good. His mother told his father about his badly-written essay, and he agreed that if Donald's work was poor because he hadn't enough time for it, then of course he must give up helping the vet. And what was more, he telephoned the vet himself, and told him that Donald was not coming any more.

The vet was very sorry. He liked Donald – he liked the way he did his work with the animals, and he would miss him. And what about that little kitten? He must find a good home for it. A pity that boy had no pets of his own, he was marvellous with animals!

Donald was very unhappy. He missed going to

the vet's. He missed the companionship of all the animals, so friendly and lively. He began to sleep badly at nights.

One night he lay awake for hours, thinking of the five dogs, the cats and the little kitten with the half-tail. He wouldn't be able to see the kitten any more and he somehow couldn't help feeling that it ought to belong to him.

He sat up in bed and looked out towards the hill where the vet lived. "I've a good mind to dress and go up to the kennels," he thought. "The dogs will know me – they won't bark. They'll be very glad to see me. They don't mind if I'm no good at sums or essays. I'm quite good enough for them. They think I'm wonderful. I'm not, of course, but it is so nice to be thought wonderful by somebody!"

He dressed quickly and slipped quietly down the stairs. He let himself out by the back door, locking it after him, and taking the key in case a burglar should try to get in.

"Now for the dogs!" he thought, feeling his heart lighter already. "They'll be so surprised and pleased! I'll feel better after I've been with them for a little while. Oh dear – sometimes I think that dogs are nicer than people!"

9

In the Middle of the Night

Donald wheeled his bicycle quietly out of the shed, and was soon speeding along the dark roads, and up the hill to where the vet lived. "I'll just have half an hour with the dogs," he thought. "I'll feel much better when I've had a word with them, and felt their tongues licking me lovingly."

He was soon at the familiar gate and rode in quietly. He put his bicycle into an empty shed, and went towards the kennels. Would the dogs bark and give the alarm, telling the vet that someone was about in the night? Or would they know his footsteps and keep quiet?

The dogs were asleep – but every one of them awoke almost as soon as Donald rode into the drive! Prince, the big Alsatian, growled and then stopped, his ears pricked up. A familiar smell came on the wind to him – a nice, clean boy-smell – the smell of that boy who looked after him a week or so ago! The Alsatian gave a little whine of joy.

The corgi was wide awake too, listening. He didn't growl. He felt sure it was the kind boy he liked so much. He tried to peer under his gate, but all he could see was the grass outside. Then he heard Donald's voice and his tail at once began to wag.

Soon Donald was peering over the gates of the dogs' kennels. The Alsatian went nearly mad with joy, but gave only a small bark of welcome for Donald shushed him as soon as he saw him.

"Sh! Don't bark! You'll wake the vet. I'll come into each of your kennels and talk to you. I've missed you so!"

He went first into the Alsatian's kennel, and the dog almost knocked him over in his joy at seeing Donald. He could not help giving a few small barks of delight. He licked the boy all over, and pawed him, and rubbed his head against him. Donald stroked and patted, and even hugged him.

"It's so lovely to be with you again," he said. "I've missed you all so. I'm in disgrace, but you don't mind, do you? Now, calm down a bit – I'm going to see the other dogs. I'll come and say goodbye to you before I go!"

He left the Alsatian's kennel and went to the next one. The corgi was there, his tail wagging nineteen to the dozen, his tongue waiting to lick Donald lovingly. The boy hugged him and tickled him and rolled him over. The corgi always loved that, for he had a great sense of fun.

Then into the next kennel, where the little poodle went nearly frantic with joy. She leaped straight into his arms, and covered his face with licks. She had missed him very much. Donald sighed happily. What a lot of love dogs had to give!

Then out he went, and into the next kennel belonging to the mongrel dog. He had gone nearly mad when he had heard Donald in the other kennels, talking to the Alsatian, the corgi and the poodle. He threw himself at the boy and began to bark for joy.

"Sh!" said Donald, in alarm. "You'll wake everybody, and I'll get into trouble. SHHH!"

The mongrel understood at once. He was a most intelligent dog, as mongrels so often are, and he certainly didn't want to get Donald into trouble. He calmed down and contented himself with licking every single bare part of Donald he could find – hands, face and neck!

"I do wish I'd thought of bringing a towel with me," said Donald, wiping his face with his hanky. "Now calm down – I'm going to see the Labrador next door to you!"

But when he shone his torch into the next kennel, the Labrador wasn't there. Another dog was there, a beautiful black, silky spaniel, the

loveliest one that Donald had ever seen. He shone his torch on her and she gave a little whine. She didn't know Donald. Who was this strange boy that all the other dogs seemed to welcome so lovingly?

"Oh – the Labrador's gone back home, I suppose," said Donald, disappointed. "But what a lovely little thing you are! And what have you got there? Tiny puppies! Let me come in and see them. I promise not to frighten them."

The spaniel listened to the boy's quiet voice and liked it. She gave a small whine as if to say, "Well, come in if you like. I'm proud of my little family!"

So Donald opened the gate and went in. The spaniel was a little wary at first, but Donald knew enough of dogs to stand perfectly still for a minute while she sniffed him all over, even standing up on her hind legs to reach to his chest. Then she gave a tiny bark that meant "Pass, friend. All's well!" and licked his right hand with her smooth tongue.

She went to her litter of tiny puppies and stood by them, looking up as if to say, "Well? Aren't they beautiful?"

"Yes, they are. And so are you," said Donald, stroking the smooth, silky head of the proud spaniel. "You must be the valuable spaniel that the vet told me was soon being sent to him, to have her puppies. He said you are worth a lot of money, and that your puppies would be worth a lot too. Oh, I wish I'd been here when you came, and could have looked after you, and cleaned your kennel and given you water."

The spaniel curled herself round her litter of puppies and looked up happily at Donald. He gave her one last pat. "Goodnight. I'll leave you in peace with your little black pups."

He went out of the kennel and saw the Alsatian still standing with his paws on the top of his kennel-gate, listening for him. "I'll just come in again and keep you company for a little while," said the boy and, to the dog's delight, he went into the kennel and sat down in the straw beside the big dog.

He laid his head on the dog's shoulder and Prince sat quite still, very happy. It was warm in the kennel, and quiet.

Donald's eyes slowly shut.

10

A Shock for Donald

Donald was fast asleep. He was warm and comfortable and happy. The big Alsatian kept very still, glad to feel the sleeping boy so near him, his ears pricked for the slightest sound. He felt as if he were guarding Donald.

Suddenly he began to growl. It was a very soft growl at first, for he did not want to disturb the boy. But soon the growl grew louder and woke Donald.

"What is it? What's the matter?" he asked Prince, who was now standing up, the hackles on his neck rising as he growled even more fiercely. Then he barked, and the sudden angry noise made Donald jump.

"What's up?" he said. "For goodness sake don't bring the vet out — he may not like my coming up here at night!"

But now the Alsatian was barking without ceasing, standing up with his feet on the gate, wishing he could jump over it. A stranger was about, and the great dog was giving warning!

"I'd better go," thought Donald. "If the vet comes and finds me here, he may think it was I who disturbed the dogs. Gracious, they're all barking now! Can there possibly be anyone about? But why? No thief could steal one of these dogs — they would fly at him at once!"

The corgi was barking his head off, and so was the mongrel dog. Even the little poodle was yapping as loudly as she could. Only the black spaniel was quiet. Perhaps she was guarding her puppies, and didn't want to frighten them.

Donald climbed over the Alsatian's gate, afraid that if he opened it the great dog would rush out, and it might be very, very difficult to get him back! He was amazed to see somebody coming out of the spaniel's kennel gate! There was very little moon that night, and all the boy could see was a dark figure, shutting the gate behind him.

"There's two of them!" said Donald to himself, as he saw someone else nearby. "What are they doing? Good gracious, surely they can't be stealing the spaniel's puppies? Where's my torch? I must go to her kennel at once!"

The two dark shadows had now disappeared silently into the bushes. Donald took his torch from his pocket and switched it on. He ran to the spaniel's kennel and shone the light into it.

"The spaniel's still there," he thought, "lying quite still as if she's asleep. I'd better go in and see if all her puppies are beside her."

So in he went, and shone his torch on to the sleeping dog. Alas, not one single puppy was beside her! She lay there alone, head on paws, eyes shut.

"How can she sleep with all this row going on, every single dog barking the place down!" thought Donald. "She must be ill!"

He touched the dog – she was warm, and he felt her breath on his hands. He shook her. "Wake up! Someone has taken your puppies! Oh dear, those men must have knocked you out! They were afraid you'd bite them, I suppose! Wake up!"

But the spaniel slept on. Donald stood up and wondered what to do. The thieves had a good start now – he wouldn't be able to catch them. But wait, he knew someone who could trail them, someone who wouldn't stop until he had caught up with the wicked thieves!

He rushed back to the Alsatian's kennel. The dog was still barking, as were all the others. "Prince, Prince, you're to go after those men!" shouted Donald, swinging open the great gate. "Get them, boy, get them! Run, then, RUN!"

The great Alsatian shot off like an arrow from a

bow, bounding along, barking fiercely. He
disappeared into the darkness, the trail of the
thieves fresh to his nose. Ah – wherever they had
gone, wherever they hid, the Alsatian would find
them!

Donald suddenly found his knees shaking, and
he felt astonished. "I'm not frightened! I suppose
it's all the excitement. Oh, those lovely puppies! I
do hope we get them back!"

And then somebody came up at a run, and caught hold of him. "What are you doing here? Why have you roused the dogs! You deserve to be punished!"

It was the vet! He couldn't see that the boy he had caught was Donald. He gave him a good shaking and Donald fell to the ground when he had finished.

"Don't, please don't!" he cried, struggling up. "I'm Donald, not a thief. Sir, thieves have been here tonight and stolen the spaniel's puppies, and . . ."

"What! Those wonderful pups!" shouted the vet, and rushed to the spaniel's kennel. He shone a powerful torch there. "I must get the police. I heard the dogs barking and came as soon as I could. But what on earth are you doing here at this time of night?"

"I couldn't sleep so I just came up to be with the dogs," said Donald. "I know it sounds silly, but it's true. I've missed them so. And I fell asleep in the Alsatian's kennel, and only woke up when the thieves came. They got away before I could do anything."

The vet shone his torch in the direction of Prince's kennel. "The door's open!" he cried. "The dog's gone!"

"Yes. I let him out, to go after the thieves," said

Donald. "You told me once that Alsatians are often used as police dogs — for tracking people — and I thought he might catch the thieves."

"Donald, you're a marvel!" said the vet, and to the boy's surprise, he felt a friendly clap on his back. "Best thing you could have done! He'll track the thieves all right and bring them back here. I wouldn't be those men for anything! Now — we'll just ring up the police and then make ourselves comfortable in Prince's kennel and wait for him to come trotting up with those two wicked men! Ha — they're going to get a very unpleasant surprise!"

11

Good Old Prince!

It was very exciting, sitting in Prince's kennel in the dark, waiting for the Alsatian to come back. The vet and Donald were not the only two waiting there – two burly policemen were there also!

The vet had telephoned the police station and the sergeant and a policeman had driven up at once, as soon as they heard what had happened. "Good idea of that boy's, to send the dog after them," said one man. "Very smart. Wish I had a dog like that!"

The other dogs were awake and restless, especially the spaniel, who missed her puppies and whined miserably. The men in the Alsatian's kennel talked quietly and Donald listened, half-wondering whether this could all be a dream. Then suddenly the mongrel gave a small, quiet bark.

"That's a warning bark," said the vet, in a low tone. "Shouldn't be surprised if Prince has found those men already, and is on his way back with them."

Soon the other dogs barked too, and the two

policemen stood up, and went silently into the dog-yard. The vet and Donald stood up too. The boy felt his knees beginning to shake with excitement again. He heard a fierce growl not far off, and a sharp bark. Yes – that was Prince all right! And what was that groaning, stumbling noise?

"That's the dog coming," said the vet, "and by the sound of it, he's got the men. I can hear them stumbling through the wood. I only hope they've brought back the pups."

As the stumbling footsteps grew nearer, the police moved forward, and shone a powerful torch into the nearby bushes. The beams picked out two terrified men and a great dog behind, his teeth bared, and a continuous growl coming from his throat – Prince, the Alsatian! He had followed the trail of the men for a mile and caught up with them! How frightened they must have been when he rounded them up!

"Stand where you are!" said the sergeant's voice, sharply. "You're under arrest. Where are the puppies?"

"Look here – that brute of a dog has bitten me!" said one of the men, holding out a bleeding hand. "I want a doctor."

"You can wait," said the sergeant. "A police van will be up here in a few minutes, and I'll take you

down to the police station, both of you. Where are the puppies?"

"We don't know," said the other man, sullenly. "We dropped them when we found this dog chasing us. Goodness knows where they are!"

"That dog's a dangerous one," said the other man, eyeing Prince carefully. "He nipped my friend too – on the leg."

"Serves you right," said the vet. "Look, Sergeant, I've got to find those pups or they'll all die. They need their mother. Will you see to these men and I'll go off with Prince and see if he can find the pups for me."

"May I come too?" asked Donald, eagerly.

"Yes. You may as well see this night's adventure to the very end!" said the vet, taking the boy's arm. "He's done well, hasn't he, Sergeant?"

"My word he has!" said the man. "Pity he's not in the police force! Maybe you will be some day, young fellow."

"I shan't," said Donald. "I'm going to be a vet. I could train police dogs for you then, if you like!"

That made everyone laugh. Then the vet gave the boy a little push. "Come on, old son – we've got to find those puppies within an hour or so or we may lose one or two of them. They'll be scared, and very hungry. Prince! Go find, Prince! Find the spaniel puppies." The black spaniel, still wide awake, was surprised at all the noise, and sad at the loss of her tiny puppies.

She suddenly gave a sharp bark. "She says she wants to come too," said Donald.

"Right. We'll take her," said the vet, and the little company set off through the bushes – first Prince the Alsatian, then the vet with a basket, then Donald, then the spaniel, nosing behind.

"How will Prince know where those men threw down the puppies?" asked Donald, as they went through the woods, the vet's torch throwing a bright beam before them.

"Well, he must have passed near them when he trailed those men," said the vet. "He'll remember all right. You can't beat an Alsatian for tracking man or animal! Hi, Prince – don't go too fast. The spaniel can't keep up with us!"

Prince went steadily on his way, standing still at times to sniff the air. After he had gone about half a mile he stopped. The spaniel gave an exited bark and ran forward.

"Prince has smelled the pups," said the vet. "So has the spaniel. Don't go any further. Let her go forward to them first."

The spaniel forced her way through the undergrowth, barking excitedly. Then she

271

suddenly stopped and nosed something, whining in delight. The vet shone his torch on her – and there, in the grass, lay the puppies, every one of them! The mother licked them lovingly and then looked up at the vet. She turned back and tried to pick up one of the pups in her mouth. She must carry it home!

"It's all right, old lady," said the vet, in the same special "animal" voice that Donald so often used. "It's all right. I've brought a basket, look – with a warm rug inside. You shall watch me put all the pups into it, and when I carry the basket you can walk back home with your nose touching it. They'll be safe – and you will soon be back in your kennel with them."

And then off went a little procession through the dark woods. First, Prince, very pleased with himself. Then the vet with the basket of pups. Then the spaniel, her nose touching the basket all the time. And last of all a very happy, excited boy – Donald. What a night! And oh, what a good thing it was that he hadn't been able to sleep and had slipped up to the kennels! That was very lucky.

12

A Surprise for Donald

When the vet, Donald, and the dogs, at last arrived back at the kennels, the telephone was ringing. The vet sighed.

"I hope it's not someone to say they want me to go and look at a sick cat, or a moping rabbit!" he said. "It's still the middle of the night, and I'm tired. Aren't you, Donald?"

"I am a bit," said Donald. "But I don't mind. It's been – well, quite an adventurous night, hasn't it?"

The vet went to the phone. "Hello? Yes. Who is it? Oh, Donald's father! Yes, actually, Donald is here. I'm sorry you were worried. Er – well, apparently he couldn't sleep, so he popped up to be with my dogs. Good thing he did, too. We've had an exciting night – been after thieves and caught them too. Donald's been quite a hero. Well, the boy's tired out now. Shall I give him a bed for the night? Yes, yes – I'd be glad to have him. Right. Goodnight!"

"Gracious – was that Dad?" said Donald, alarmed. "Was he very angry because I'd come up here in the middle of the night?"

"No. No, I don't think so," said the vet. "He seemed very relieved to know you were here, safe and sound. You get off to bed, old son. You can have the room next to mine. Don't bother about washing or anything – you're tired out. Just flop into bed."

Donald fell asleep almost at once. He was tired out, as the vet had said, but very happy. What a good thing he had come up to the kennels and had spotted those thieves! What a good thing that Prince had found those lovely little spaniel puppies! What a good thing that . . . but just then he fell fast asleep, and slept so very soundly that he didn't even stir until the vet came to wake him the next morning.

"Oh goodness – shall I be late for school?" said Donald, looking in alarm at his watch.

"No. Calm down. It's Saturday!" said the vet. "Your mother's been on the phone this morning – she sounds very excited about something. I won't tell you what! She says will you please come back in time for breakfast."

"Oh dear, I hope I'm not going to get into any more trouble!" said Donald, jumping out of bed.

"No, I don't somehow think you'll find trouble waiting for you!" said the vet. "Buck up, though –

and come back and help me today if you're allowed to."

Donald dressed at top speed and shot home on his bicycle. Would his father be angry with him for slipping away in the middle of the night? Well – it had been worth it! It was a pity he hadn't been able to go and see if the spaniel puppies were all well and happy this morning, but maybe he could come back later on in the day.

He arrived home, put his bicycle away, and ran in through the kitchen door. As soon as he went into the sitting-room, his mother ran to meet him and gave him a hug.

"Donald! Oh Donald, I didn't know I had such a brave son!"

"Well done, my boy!" said his father, and clapped him on the back. "Fancy you being in the papers!"

Donald was astonished. He stared at his father, puzzled. "What do you mean, Dad?"

"Well, look here!" said his father, and showed him the first page of his newspaper – and there, right in the middle, was a paragraph all about Donald!

BOY SENDS ALSATIAN DOG AFTER THIEVES

IN MIDDLE OF NIGHT

HELPS POLICE TO FIND VALUABLE SPANIEL PUPPIES

And then came the story of how Donald had gone up to the kennels in the middle of the night, heard the thieves, sent the Alsatian after them – and all the rest!

"I suppose the police told the paper all that last night," said Donald, astonished. "I couldn't sleep for thinking of those dogs, that's why I went up to them in the middle of the night. I know you said I wasn't to go and help the vet – but I did so want to see the dogs again. I just felt sort of lonely."

"Well, all's well that ends well," said his father, feeling really very pleased with Donald. "Your mother and I are proud of you. We've been talking things over, and we're both agreed that you shall go and help the vet again . . ."

"Oh Dad! Thank you!" cried Donald, his heart jumping for joy. "Now I'll be able to see those

276

spaniel puppies again that the thieves took. Oh, they're beautiful! Oh, I wish I was rich enough to buy one! Oh, and that little kitten too. I wish I was rich enough to pay the vet to keep it for me! I wish I could buy a . . ."

"Well now, that's enough, Donald," said his father. "It's no good getting big ideas, especially while your schoolwork is poor."

"What about your homework for the week-end?" said his mother. "You mustn't forget that, in all the excitement! What have you to do? Sums? An essay? Geography or history?"

"I've forgotten," said Donald, feeling suddenly down-hearted. "Bother it! Where did I put my exercise book? The homework I've to do for the weekend is written there. I don't feel at all like doing any!"

He fetched his exercise book and turned to the page where the instructions for his weekend homework were written down. "Here it is – oh no, an essay again! 'Write down what you would like to be when you grow up, and give the reasons why.'" Donald stared at it in sudden delight. "I can do that! I want to be a vet, of course, and I know all the reasons why. I can put dogs and cats and horses and birds and everything into this essay. I'll write it at once, this very minute!"

13

A Wonderful Day

It was really very surprising to see Donald settling down so very happily to do his homework. "We usually have such silly, dull things to write about," he said. "Now this is sensible. I've plenty to say! I only hope there are enough pages to say it in."

It was while Donald was finishing the longest essay in his life that there came a knock at the door. It was a man from another newspaper, wanting to ask questions about Donald and his exciting night.

"I'm sorry," said his father. "The boy has had enough excitement. We don't want him to talk to newspaper men, and get conceited about himself."

"Oh, I only want to ask him a few questions," said the man. "Such as, what does he plan to be when he's grown up? Maybe a policeman, perhaps, catching thieves and the like?"

Donald, writing his essay, heard all this. He ran to the door. "That's exactly what I'm writing for my weekend essay!" he said, surprised. "I'm going to be a vet, of course. I'm putting down all my reasons. I've just finished!"

"And what are your reasons?" asked the man, smiling at Donald.

"Now listen," said Donald's father, pushing the boy away. "We've told you that we don't want our son to think himself too clever for words, and to get conceited! The most we'll let you do is to read what he has written."

"Let me just have a look at it, then," said the man. Donald handed the exercise book to him and the man glanced quickly down the essay.

"Good, good, good!" he said. "Best essay I've read for ages – straight from the heart – you mean every word of it, don't you, youngster? Do you get top marks every week for your essays? You ought to."

"No. I'm pretty well always bottom," said Donald. "But this is different. It's something I like writing about, something I want to write about. I know all about a vet's work, you see. It's great."

"Go away now, Donald," said his father, anxious not to let the boy talk too much. "Leave your essay with me." Donald went off, and his father turned to the waiting newspaper man.

"You can have this essay of his, instead of talking to him, if you like. But I think you should pay the lad for it, you know, if you want to print it. I'll put the money into the bank for him."

"Right. Here's a hundred pounds," said the man, much to the astonishment of Donald's father. "And if that form master of his marks him bottom for this essay, well, all I can say is, the man doesn't know his job! I'll take it with me, have it copied, and send back the essay in time for him to take it to school next week. Thank you, sir. Good-day!"

And away went the man, looking very pleased with himself. "Ha!" he thought. "Fancy that kid writing such an interesting piece about a vet's work, and all his animals – most remarkable! Good boy that. Deserves to have animals of his own. Funny there wasn't even a dog about the place – or a cat! Well, maybe the money would help him to buy a pet for himself!"

Donald's mother and father were very proud and pleased to have been given a hundred pounds for his essay. They went to tell Donald.

"Good gracious! All that for a school essay!" said the boy, astounded. "I wish I'd written it better. It isn't worth fifty pence, really. And I bet I'll be bottom in class as usual! But I say – a hundred pounds! Now – what shall I spend it on?"

"Well, I shall put it in the bank for you, of course!" said his father. The boy stared at him in dismay.

"Oh no, Dad! I want to spend it – spend it on

something I badly want! It's my money. Mum, please ask Daddy to let me have it."

"Yes. Yes, I think you should have it, dear," said his mother, very proud of all that Donald had done the night before. "Give it to him, Bob – we'll let him spend it on whatever he likes. He shall choose!"

"Whatever I like, Mum – do you really mean that?" cried Donald. "You won't say no to anything?"

"Well – you've been such a brave lad, quite a hero, and I think for once you should do as you please," said his mother.

"Mum – if I buy a puppy with it, will you say no?" asked Donald.

"I'll say yes, you deserve one," said his mother, and his father nodded his head too.

"And suppose I asked you if I could have a little hurt kitten that the vet's keeping for me – would you mind?" asked the boy. "It has only half a tail, because a dog bit it, so it's not beautiful, but I do love the little thing. That's really why I went to work for the vet – because he took the kitten and tended it, and kept it, and when he said he would send the bill to Dad, I said no, I'd work for him, and he could keep my earnings to pay for the kitten."

281

His mother suddenly put her arms round him and gave him a warm hug.

"You can have a dog, a cat, a kitten, a guinea-pig, anything you like! We didn't know quite what a clever son we had, nor how brave he is. We know better now. We're very very proud of you, Donald."

"Oh Mum! A dog of my own – a kitten! Oh, and I might get a donkey, if I save up enough. He could live in the vet's field. And I'll buy a cage and keep budgies – blue ones and green ones. Oh, I can't believe it!"

"And if Mr Fairly, that form master of yours, gives you low marks for that fine essay, I'll have something to say to him!" said Donald's father. "Well, well – I suppose we must now give up the idea of your being an architect when you grow up, Donald. It will be fun to have a vet in the family, for a change! I'm proud of you, son, I really am!"

14

Donald – and His Dog!

Donald's father kept his word. He didn't put the hundred pounds into the bank – he gave it to Donald. "Wow, how rich I am!" said the boy, delighted. "Mum, do you mind if I go up to see the vet and tell him about the money?"

"Off you go!" said his mother. "But please come back for lunch – I'm going to arrange a very special one for you!"

Donald shot off to the vet's on his bicycle. He whistled as he went, because he felt so happy. To think that last night he was so unhappy that he couldn't even go to sleep – and today he was too happy for words! All because he rushed off to see the dogs in the middle of the night!

The vet was delighted to see him again so soon and whistled in surprise when he saw the ten-pound notes that the boy showed him.

"Well, well – writing must be a paying job, if you can earn a hundred pounds for an essay!" he said. "It takes me quite a time to earn that amount!"

"Sir, could I buy one of those beautiful spaniel puppies?" said Donald, earnestly. "I want one more than anything in the world. A dog of my own — just imagine! Someone who'll understand my every word, who'll always know what I'm feeling and will never let me down, because he will be my very faithful friend."

"Well, if ever a boy deserved a dog, it's you, Donald," said the vet. "But you're not going to buy one of those pups, I'll give you one. I meant to buy one for you, anyway, for what you did last night, and for all the help you've given me. You shall choose your own pup. Come along — let's see which one you want, before anyone else has their pick."

Donald was speechless. His face went bright red, and the vet laughed. "Can't you say a single word? And there's another thing — that little kitten is well enough to go now. I know you want her. You should have her too. Let her and the pup grow up together."

"Thank you, thank you!" said Donald, finding his tongue. "But please, I've plenty of money now! I can pay you."

"I know. But if you really are going in for animals, you'll want kennels and cages and things," said the vet. "I'll show you how to make them – much cheaper than buying them – all you'll have to do is to buy the wood and the nails. You're good with your hands – you'll enjoy making things."

"It all seems rather like a dream," said Donald, as they went to look at the puppies. "I was so miserable yesterday and today I feel on top of the world! Oh I say, aren't the puppies lovely? They seem to have grown since last night. That little fellow is trying to crawl!"

The spaniel's mother looked up at them out of beautiful brown eyes. With her nose she gently pushed one of the puppies towards Donald. "That's

the one she wants you to have!" said the vet. "It's the best of the lot."

And that is the one Donald chose. He left it with the mother till it was old enough to be his – and now he is making a splendid kennel for it! "It will be yours when you are old enough," he tells the puppy. "I expect the kitten will sometimes sleep in your kennel with you, so I'll bring her along soon so that you can make friends."

He went to tell his granny about the dog he had chosen. She listened, very pleased. "Well, well, I meant to give you a puppy myself, for your birthday, if your mother said yes – and now you have won one for yourself, by working for the vet. You deserve a dog, Donald, and I know you'll train him well. I can't give you a dog, now you have one – so I think I'll buy you a really good dog basket, so that you can have her in your room at night, to guard you when you're asleep!"

"That puppy is going to be very lucky!" said Donald. "I'm making her a lovely kennel – the vet's helping me. We went and bought the wood together, out of the money I was given for that essay. I have a kitten too – the one whose tail was half bitten off by a dog. And I think I'm going to breed budgerigars, Granny. I've still enough money out of my hundred pounds to buy a breeding cage.

I'm going to give you my first baby budgie. Would you like a green or a blue one?"

"Oh – a green one, I think," said Granny. "It will match my curtains! Bless you, Donald, you do deserve your good luck. You earned it yourself, and that's the best good luck there is!"

Donald still goes up to help the vet, of course, and you should have seen him one week when the vet was ill! He looked after all the dogs, the cats, the birds – and a little sick monkey! How happy and proud he was! How good it felt to go round and see every animal, big or small, look up in delight when he came.

Prince, the Alsatian, has gone back to his own home now, of course – but Donald often sees him when he goes out. Prince always sees him first, though! Donald suddenly hears a soft galloping noise behind him and then he almost falls over as the big Alsatian flings himself on the boy, whining and licking, pawing him lovingly.

"Do you still remember that exciting night in the dark woods?" says Donald, ruffling the thick fur round the dog's neck. "Remember those little spaniel puppies? Do you see this beautiful black spaniel at my heels – she was one of the pups we rescued that night, you and I! I chose her for myself. Dear old Prince. I'll never forget you!"

One day you may meet a boy walking over the grassy hills somewhere — a boy with five or six dogs round him, dogs that come at his slightest whistle. It will be Donald, taking out the kennel-dogs for the vet, letting them race and leap and play to their hearts' content.

You'll know which is his dog without him telling you — that silky black spaniel beside him. What is its name? Well, call "Bonny, Bonny, Bonny" and it will come rushing over to you at once!